Grimmer Folk Stories

By

John Doriot

Grimmer Folk Stories

This is a work of fiction. All of the characters, organizations, and events are either products of the author's imagination or are used fictitiously.

ISBN 978-1-7352483-4-9

Dedication

For Nolan – The best of friends for forty-eight years and counting....

Preface

Jacob and Wilhelm Grimm published their first volume of fairy tales over two hundred years ago. The modern versions of these stories have become beloved movies that are still viewed today, and tales that have been read countless times to children as "bedtime stories." Believe me when I say this, you would not want to read the original version of the story to your children. In fact, I was shocked when I began reading the unmodified stories first published in the early 1800s. The original versions are not stories for children unless you dislike children, but believe it or not, that's how they were sold and offered to the public. I am surprised any child that was read one of these stories ever went to sleep.

Don't believe me? Let me give you several good examples. Remember Cinderella? In the original Grimm story, one of her stepsisters cuts off her big toe to fit into the lost slipper and the other one cuts off part of her heel, but the prince sees that the shoe doesn't fit anyone except his one true love, Cinderella. And just to tidy things up at the end, the prince is told what the stepsisters had done to try and fit in the shoe by two pigeons at the wedding, who then peck out the eyes of the two stepsisters because of their wickedness and dishonesty. Recall, Snow White? Well, in the original story, she has a wicked stepmother (man, the Grimm boys didn't like stepmothers), who was forced to wear shoes with hot coals in them, running around in circles until she falls down dead. Now granted, I think they all had it coming, but I wasn't writing a book or a screenplay for a movie for children. And if you haven't already guessed, I am not this time either.

The stories known as Grimm's fairy tales have had figurative childproof locks applied to their pages by smart writers using fairy dust and a knowledge that within those stories were indeed vivid tales full of imagination that just needed a little "tweaking." All but maybe one - Hansel and Gretel. I mean, it's difficult to ignore the fact that the woman in the forest is a cannibal who likes to eat children and they kill her by throwing her into the oven. It's hard to overcome that plotline with animation and/or talking animals.

But unlike the child-friendly versions, I wrote these folk stories as I think the Grimm Brothers would have preferred. I mean, why cut off a toe when you can cut off a head? And just to show you what I mean, I have provided you the original version of each Grimm folk tale followed by my version of that same story. As I said, I don't recommend reading these stories to children, unless you want them to have nightmares. Then by all means......

Table of Contents

The Singing Bone

Once upon a time in a certain country, there was great concern about a wild boar that was destroying the peasants' fields, killing the cattle, and ripping people apart with its tusks. The king promised a large reward to anyone who could free the land from this plague, but the beast was so large and strong that no one dared to go near the woods where it lived. Finally, the king proclaimed that whoever could capture or kill the wild boar should have his only daughter in marriage.

Now in this country there lived two brothers, sons of a poor man. They declared that they dared to attempt the task. The older one, who was crafty and shrewd, did so out of pride. The younger one, who was innocent and simple, did so because of his kind heart.

The king said, "To be more sure of finding the beast, you should enter the woods from opposite sides." Thus, the older one entered the woods from the west and the younger one from the east.

After the younger one had walked a little while, a little dwarf stepped up to him. He held a black spear in his hand and said, "I am giving you this spear because your heart is innocent and good. With it, you can confidently attack the wild boar. It will do you no harm."

He thanked the dwarf, put the spear on his shoulder, and walked on fearlessly. Before long he saw the beast. It attacked him, but he held the spear toward it, and in its blind fury it ran into the

1

spear with such force that its heart was slashed in two. Then he put the monster on his back and turned towards home, intending to take it to the king.

Emerging from the other side of the woods, he came to a house where people were making merry, drinking wine, and dancing. His older brother was there too. Thinking that the boar would not run away from him any time soon, he had decided to drink himself some real courage. When he saw his younger brother coming out of the woods with his booty, his envious and evil heart gave him no peace.

He called out to him, "Come in, dear brother. Rest and refresh yourself with a beaker of wine."

The younger brother, suspecting no evil, went in and told him about the good dwarf who had given him the spear with which he had killed the boar. The older brother kept him there until evening, and then they set forth together. After dark, they came to a bridge over a brook, and the older brother let the younger one go first. When the younger brother reached the middle above the water, the older one gave him such a blow from behind that he fell dead.

He buried him beneath the bridge, took the boar, and delivered it to the king, pretending that he had killed it. With this, he received the king's daughter in marriage.

When his younger brother did not return he said, "The boar must have ripped him apart," and everyone believed it.

But as nothing remains hidden from God, this black deed was also to come to light. After many long years, a shepherd was driving his herd across the bridge and saw a little snow-white bone lying in the sand below. Thinking that it would make a good mouthpiece, he climbed down, picked it up, and then carved out of it a mouthpiece for his horn. When he blew into it for the first time, to his great astonishment the bone began to sing by itself:

Oh, my dear shepherd,
You are blowing on my little bone.
My brother killed me,
And buried me beneath the bridge,
To get the wild boor
For the daughter of the king.

"What a wonderful horn," said the shepherd. "It sings by itself. I must take it to the king."

When he brought it before the king, the horn again began to sing its little song. The king understood it well and had the earth beneath the bridge dug up. Then the whole skeleton of the murdered man came to light.

The wicked brother could not deny the deed. He was sewn into a sack and drowned alive. The murdered man's bones were laid to rest in a beautiful grave in the churchyard.

Good Bones

Once upon a time in a very dark alley, a man lay looking up at the sky. His eyes were the color of Tabasco sauce and often burned and were blurry. But this particular night, the moon and the stars did not appear as dull reflections seen from a mirror. No, this night they shouted down to him with a bright voice and urged him to listen.

The face of the moon, which scientists say is created by the light and dark areas of the lunar surface, appeared more human that night. So human that to James, it appeared to be staring at him with its eyes and face suggesting a grim demeanor.

"James, you are killing yourself and in doing so, you killed another."

"Fuck off," James replied in the eloquent manner he used whenever his heroin blanket was pulled away by someone or something within his alley.

A man who James knew well and was allowed in his alley stumbled over next to him and fell against the building, sliding down the wall until his butt and the alley pavement stopped his descent.

"Do you see that, Stick? That damn big moon and its face. Looking down at us."

Stick didn't reply immediately but James was used to that. It often took several minutes before Stick was able to decipher the question and process enough of it to be able to respond. It could also be one of those nights when Stick didn't answer to anyone. James was hoping it was one of those delayed response evenings as opposed to the latter.

"The moon. Yeah. man. I see it, dude. Shit. He sure looks pissed. What the hell did you do, Jimmy, to make him so mad?"

Damn, he can see it too. I wonder if he can hear it talk.

"What do you mean I killed another?"

"I didn't say you killed anyone," Stick answered.

4

"No shit, man. I was talking to the moon. Shut up for a minute. Well, I'm waiting, Mr. High and Mighty. My friend Stick is here now. Tell him what you just said."

"You understand the words. I do not need to explain what they mean."

"Did you hear that, Stick? Did you hear what that fucker said to me?"

"Hear who?"

"Hell. Never mind, Stick. Never mind."

Shit. He just sees the fucking moon. KInda hard not to see it on a night like this. It fills up the damn sky. Where did all the stars go? Now, it just seems like a black curtain with some gigantic nickel looking down at me. What president is on the nickel? Washington?

"Is that you, George?" James yelled as he began to laugh.

"No man, it's me, Stick. Jimmy, it's Stick."

"Shut up, Stick! Me and George are talking now. Up there in the sky. That ain't no damn moon. It's a gigantic-ass nickel. See that face on that big giant nickel staring down at us? It's George Washington. He's talking to me."

"Jefferson," Stick said before his head fell back against the wall. One of the scabs on the back of his head came loose and blood trickled down his neck.

"Jefferson? What the hell are you talking about, you drunk son of a bitch?"

"Jefferson is on the nickel, Jimmy, not Washington," Stick explained as he toppled over.

James looked at Stick who was now slumped over with his head laying on a pile of trash.

"God damn!" he exclaimed and jerked back when he saw Stick's eye come out of his head. As he strained to focus, he realized it was only a cockroach that had come crawling out of the bag of trash onto his face.

"Hello, Every Fucking Body!" James yelled and laughed. He closed his eyes and saw the face of the nickel and remembered. It was Jefferson, just like Stick said before he passed out. *George Washington. He's on the quarter* he said to himself. He opened his eyes and looked back up in the sky.

"Hell, looks more like a quarter anyway, so I was right. It is you, isn't it, George? What the fuck do you want?"

"I want you to remember."

5

"Sorry, George. Shop is closed for repairs right now." James started laughing again. "Come back tomorrow," he said as his eyes changed into glassy marbles and he seemed to float for a moment up off the ground. He felt someone kick his feet and thought it was Stick. He threw his arm out at him and hit his shoulder.

"God dammit, Stick. Leave me the hell alone."

He felt the kick again and when he opened his eyes, he saw the face of George glaring at him. It seemed to be right in front of him and he had to turn his head because the glimmering silver was so bright. He reached into his pocket and felt for the knife that he needed for protection to live in his environment. He pulled it out and released the trigger, exposing the sharp pointed blade. He pushed up and out with his arm without looking but he felt nothing, so he moved his arm back and forth several times. He encountered no resistance against the blade and heard no screams from anyone that may have felt its pointed nature. He opened his eyes and the face was still there. Just as big and just as stern, staring down at him.

Man, you are totally messed up, tonight. Just close your eyes and enjoy the feeling. You've had hallucinations before and this is only another one, so just go with it.

"Yeah, fuck you, George," James said as he closed his eyes and sensed his spirit floating above him.

"Cool," he said as he saw his own body lying there next to Stick. George was gone and he smiled at the aroma of the food from the Chinese restaurant that was near the alley. He floated toward the smell and watched several customers go in the door.

"Hey man, get me some moo goo gai pan!" he yelled but the people below him didn't respond.

He laughed as he said the words over and over in his head. *I wonder if that's what Chinese cows sound like* he thought as he laughed again. He floated through the city, looking down at several familiar sites associated with his alley. There was the Wooden Nickel bar that still allowed him in, even though they usually ended up throwing him out before the night was over. He heard the bell of the Golden Dragon pawn shop door as it opened and closed. He had been cussed out by the owner on more than one occasion when he was very high for standing next to the door and flicking the bell so he could listen to it.

If he wasn't such a good customer, not only as a seller but as a buyer, he would have been banned from the establishment. He

6

lingered there for a few moments hoping someone would open the door again and when someone finally did, he moved on. He saw the Princess strip club and thought how glad he was that several of the girls that worked there liked to get as high as he did because it provided him an opportunity to have sex; at least when he was able to do so.

He floated further down the street and into another area that made him uneasy because he only went there to beg for money or try and steal something. He had stayed away from that place for several weeks now, ever since he found the money. And as soon as he thought about the money, he found himself in his house. Lying in his old bed, with his twin brother Joseph sitting next to him, feeding him some soup.

His brother had brought him back to the house after he found him beaten up in the alley. Joseph had always tried to help him. Gave him money, food, clothing. Tried to encourage him to seek professional help and several times he did. But his destructive nature would always suppress the affirmations or truth that the counselors provided and he would end up finding the world that didn't disappoint him. The one that allowed him to escape the envy he carried deep inside of him and made him hate the success of his brother.

He saw Joseph confronting him as he held his father's silver and gold coin collection and heard him tell him to put it back, that he would give him some money. He heard himself scream he didn't want his "god damn money or pity" before he threw down the coins and grabbed his brother's head and twisted it so hard that his neck snapped. He saw himself dragging his brother's body into the woods behind their house and burying his body deep in the cave where they used to play when they were younger.

And then he saw George again. Staring down at him. Screaming at him. Yelling at him. "I knew it was you all the time; I just wanted to hear you say it!" As soon as he heard those words, he felt himself getting sick. He threw up again and again and began to choke. He clawed at his throat, attempting to get air into his lungs but his throat and lungs were full of vomit and bile. The rest of his body was too weak to overcome the sickening assault, so his body convulsed as it was deprived of oxygen. The last thing he saw was Stick's body and a face that looked familiar before his brain turned off his body's autonomic survival mechanism and he died.

James's father found Joseph's body and provided it a proper burial. Two weeks later, the police came to his house to inform him they had found his son's decomposing body in an alley. James's father said his other son had died many years ago and closed the door.

The Devil with the Three Golden Hairs

O nce upon a time, a poor woman gave birth to a little son; and as he came into the world with a caul on, it was predicted that in his fourteenth year he would have the King's daughter for his wife. It happened that soon afterward the King came into the village, and no one knew that he was the King, and when he asked the people what news there was, they answered, "A child has just been born with a caul on; whatever any one so born undertakes turns out well. It is prophesied, too, that in his fourteenth year he will have the King's daughter for his wife."

The King, who had a bad heart, and was angry about the prophecy, went to the parents, and, seeming quite friendly, said, "You poor people, let me have your child, and I will take care of it." At first, they refused, but when the stranger offered them a large amount of gold for it, and they thought, "It is a luck-child, and everything must turn out well for it." They at last consented and gave him the child.

The King put it in a box and rode away with it until he came to a deep piece of water; then he threw the box into it and thought, "I have freed my daughter from her unlooked-for suitor." The box, however, did not sink but floated like a boat, and not a drop of water made its way into it. And it floated to within two miles of the King's chief city, where there was a mill, and it came to a stand-still at the mill-dam. A miller's boy, who by good luck was standing there, noticed it and pulled it out with a hook, thinking that he had found a great treasure, but when he opened it there lay a pretty boy

9

inside, quite fresh and lively. He took him to the miller and his wife, and as they had no children, they were glad, and said, "God has given him to us." They took great care of the foundling, and he grew up in all goodness.

It happened that once in a storm the King went into the mill, and he asked the mill-folk if the tall youth was their son. "No," answered they, "he's a foundling. Fourteen years ago he floated down to the mill-dam in a box, and the mill-boy pulled him out of the water." Then the King knew that it was none other than the luck-child which he had thrown into the water, and he said, "My good people, could not the youth take a letter to the Queen; I will give him two gold pieces as a reward?"

"Just as the King commands," answered they, and they told the boy to hold himself in readiness. Then the King wrote a letter to the Queen, wherein he said, "As soon as the boy arrives with this letter, let him be killed and buried, and all must be done before I come home."

The boy set out with this letter, but he lost his way, and in the evening came to a large forest. In the darkness he saw a small light; he went towards it and reached a cottage. When he went in, an old woman was sitting by the fire quite alone. She started when she saw the boy, and said, "Whence do you come, and whither are you going?"

"I come from the mill," he answered, "and wish to go to the Queen, to whom I am taking a letter; but as I have lost my way in the forest I should like to stay here overnight."

"You poor boy," said the woman, "you have come into a den of thieves, and when they come home they will kill you."

10

"Let them come," said the boy, "I am not afraid, but I am so tired that I cannot go any farther." And he stretched himself upon a bench and fell asleep.

Soon afterward the robbers came and angrily asked what strange boy was lying there. "Ah," said the old woman, "it is an innocent child who has lost himself in the forest, and out of pity I have let him come in; he has to take a letter to the Queen." The robbers opened the letter and read it, and in it was written that the boy as soon as he arrived should be put to death. Then the hard-hearted robbers felt pity, and their leader tore up the letter and wrote another, saying, that soon as the boy came, he should be married at once to the King's daughter. Then they let him lie quietly on the bench until the next morning, and when he awoke they gave him the letter and showed him the right way.

And the Queen, when she had received the letter and read it, did as was written in it, and had a splendid wedding-feast prepared, and the King's daughter was married to the luck-child; and as the youth was handsome and agreeable she lived with him in joy and contentment.

After some time, the King returned to his palace and saw that the prophecy was fulfilled, and the luck-child was married to his daughter. "How has that come to pass?" said he; "I gave quite another order in my letter."

So, the Queen gave him the letter and said that he might see for himself what was written in it. The King read the letter and saw quite well that it had been exchanged for the other. He asked the youth what had become of the letter entrusted to him, and why he had brought another instead of it. "I know nothing about it," answered he; "it must have been changed in the night when I slept in the forest."

The King said in a passion, "You shall not have everything quite so much your own way; whosoever marries my daughter must fetch me from hell three golden hairs from the head of the devil; bring me what I want, and you shall keep my daughter." In this way, the King hoped to be rid of him forever. But the luck-child answered, "I will fetch the golden hairs, I am not afraid of the Devil." Thereupon he took leave of them and began his journey.

The road led him to a large town, where the watchman by the gates asked him what his trade was, and what he knew. "I know everything." answered the luck-child. "Then you can do us a favor," said the watchman. "If you will tell us why our market-fountain, which once flowed with wine has become dry and no longer gives even water?"

"That you shall know," answered he; "only wait until I come back." Then he went farther and came to another town, and there also the gatekeeper asked him what was his trade, and what he knew. "I know everything," answered he. "Then you can do us a favor, and tell us why a tree in our town which once bore golden apples now does not even put forth leaves?"

"You shall know that," answered he; "only wait until I come back." Then he went on and came to a wide river over which he must go. The ferryman asked him what his trade was, and what he knew. "I know everything," answered he. "Then you can do me a favor," said the ferryman, "and tell me why I must always be rowing backward and forward and am never set free?"

"You shall know that," answered he; "only wait until I come back."

When he had crossed the water, he found the entrance to Hell. It was black and sooty within, and the Devil was not at home, but his grandmother was sitting in a large armchair. "What do you want?" said she to him, but she did not look so very wicked.

12

"I should like to have three golden hairs from the devil's head," answered he, "else I cannot keep my wife."

"That is a good deal to ask for," said she; "if the devil comes home and finds you, it will cost you your life; but as I pity you, I will see if I cannot help you." She changed him into an ant and said, "Creep into the folds of my dress, you will be safe there."

"Yes," answered he, "so far, so good; but there are three things besides that I want to know: why a fountain which once flowed with wine has become dry and no longer gives even water; why a tree which once bore golden apples does not even put forth leaves; and why a ferry-man must always be going backward and forward and is never set free?"

"Those are difficult questions," answered she, "but only be silent and quiet and pay attention to what the devil says when I pull out the three golden hairs."

As the evening came on the devil returned home. No sooner had he entered than he noticed that the air was not pure. "I smell man's flesh," said he; "all is not right here." Then he pried into every corner, and searched, but could not find anything. His grandmother scolded him. "It has just been swept," said she, "and everything put in order, and now you are upsetting it again; you have always got man's flesh in your nose. Sit down and eat your supper."

When he had eaten and drunk, he was tired and laid his head in his grandmother's lap, and before long he was fast asleep, snoring and breathing heavily. Then the old woman took hold of a golden hair, pulled it out, and laid it down near her. "Oh!" cried the devil, "What are you doing?"

"I have had a bad dream," answered the grandmother, "so I seized hold of your hair."

"What did you dream then?" said the devil.

"I dreamed that a fountain in a marketplace from which wine once flowed was dried up, and not even water would flow out of it; what is the cause of it?"

"Oh, ho! If they did but know it," answered the devil; "a toad is sitting under a stone in the well; if they killed it, the wine would flow again."

He went to sleep again and snored until the windows shook. Then she pulled the second hair out. "Ha! What are you doing?" cried the devil angrily.

"Do not take it ill," said she, "I did it in a dream."

"What have you dreamt this time?" asked he.

"I dreamt that in a certain kingdom there stood an apple tree which had once borne golden apples, but now would not even bear leaves. What, think you, was the reason?"

"Oh! If they did but know." answered the devil. "A mouse is gnawing at the root; if they killed this they would have golden apples again, but if it gnaws much longer the tree will wither altogether. But leave me alone with your dreams: if you disturb me in my sleep again you will get a box on the ear."

The grandmother spoke gently to him until he fell asleep again and snored. Then she took hold of the third golden hair and pulled it out. The devil jumped up, roared out, and would have treated her ill, but she quieted him once more and said, "Who can help bad dreams?"

"What was the dream, then?" asked he, and was quite curious.

"I dreamt of a ferryman who complained that he must always ferry from one side to the other, and was never released. What is the cause of it?"

"Ah! The fool," answered the devil; "when anyone comes and wants to go across he must put the oar in his hand, and the other man will have to ferry and he will be free."

As the grandmother had plucked out the three golden hairs, and the three questions were answered, she let the old serpent alone, and he slept until daybreak.

When the devil had gone out again, the old woman took the ant out of the folds of her dress and gave the luck-child his human shape again. "There are the three golden hairs for you," said she. "What the Devil said to your three questions, I suppose you heard?"

"Yes," answered he, "I heard, and will take care to remember."

"You have what you want," said she, "and now you can go your way." He thanked the old woman for helping him in his need and left hell well content that everything had turned out so fortunately.

When he came to the ferryman he was expected to give the promised answer. "Ferry me across first," said the luck-child, "and then I will tell you how you can be set free." And when he reached the opposite shore, he gave him the devil's advice: "Next time anyone comes, who wants to be ferried over, just put the oar in his hand."

He went on and came to the town wherein stood the unfruitful tree, and there too the watchman wanted an answer. So, he told him what he had heard from the devil: "Kill the mouse which is gnawing at its root, and it will again bear golden apples." Then the watchman thanked him and gave him as a reward two asses laden with gold, which followed him.

At last, he came to the town whose well was dry. He told the watchman what the devil had said: "A toad is in the well beneath a stone; you must find it and kill it, and the well will again give wine in plenty." The watchman thanked him, and also gave him two asses laden with gold.

At last, the luck-child got home to his wife, who was heartily glad to see him again and to hear how well he had prospered in everything. To the King he took what he had asked for, the devil's three golden hairs, and when the King saw the four asses laden with gold, he was quite content, and said, "Now all the conditions are fulfilled, and you can keep my daughter. But tell me, dear son-in-law, where did all that gold come from? This is tremendous wealth!"

"I was rowed across a river," answered he, "and got it there; it lies on the shore instead of sand."

"Can I too fetch some of it?" said the King; and he was quite eager about it.

"As much as you like," answered he. "There is a ferryman on the river; let him ferry you over, and you can fill your sacks on the other side." The greedy King set out in all haste, and when he came to the river, he beckoned to the ferryman to put him across. The ferryman came and bade him get in, and when they got to the other shore he put the oar in his hand and sprang out. But from this time forth the King had to ferry, as a punishment for his sins.

Perhaps he is ferrying still? If he is, it is because no one has taken the oar from him.

The Grimalkin

Once upon a time, a man sat in a chair looking out his window. It was winter and snow covered the ground but it was no longer a pretty white snow. It was now brownish-black in many places as the dirt from the world filled in the melted voids that refroze overnight.

"It looks terribly cold out there," he said as he poured himself another glass of wine. He looked down and saw a thin gray hair on the side of the glass and brushed it off. He rubbed his hand through his hair before he took several large swallows.

"Yes, it is very cold. It is below freezing but it will get warmer as the days pass."

"I suppose so, my friend. Do you have any idea as to how long we have had snow on the ground?"

"It has been nineteen days, seventeen hours, and twenty-three minutes."

"You have a remarkable memory. Not many people would be able to remember time in that manner."

"Not many. But, what else do we have but time? We are on the top of a mountain of ice and snow that is at least two feet deep. And your car won't start. At least it wouldn't start yesterday. Have you tried it today?"

"No, not today."

"Perhaps you should try it again. Who knows? It might start if we are lucky."

"You are the eternal optimist," the man said as he got up and went out to the garage. He put the key in the ignition and turned. The engine groaned for a moment, like a dying old man trying to breathe and then the car started as if the old man had only needed his empty oxygen tank exchanged for a full one.

"I'll be damned." He smiled and took a sip of his wine.

"Told you. I brought the bottle of wine to celebrate."

"Thank you, old friend. But if I drink this wine, we will never get down the mountain."

"Well, if you turn off the car, it may never start again and then we will be stuck on this mountain for who knows how long. And once the snow and ice begin to melt, you will see things you don't want to see."

His friend was right. He wanted to be gone before the snow melted and revealed what lay beneath it. He refilled his glass as he subconsciously removed another gray hair from its side. When he glanced out the window, he thought he saw something that looked odd, right next to the large cedar tree. For a moment he thought it might be a squirrel but the more he looked the more he realized the squirrel wasn't moving. And it wasn't the right color for a squirrel. What he saw was black although it did have a white belly.

"Have you ever seen a black squirrel?"

"They are very rare. I have never seen one around here. But what I think you are seeing is the top of her head beginning to show as the ice melts. I actually think I can see some of her fingers sticking out over there next to the bird feeder. Yes. See the cardinal? I believe it just landed on top of her middle finger."

His hand began to shake as he took another drink of wine. His friend was right. He was looking at the forehead of his girlfriend. And those were her fingers the cardinal was perched upon. He couldn't remember where the rest of her body was, but he knew it was there somewhere beneath all that dirty snow. He needed to talk about something else. Anything but what he could now see from the windows of the garage door.

"It will be dark soon. I hate that it gets dark so early these days. It's depressing."

"I think it will be best to leave in the dark though, don't you? Would you like for me to get your pills?"

"Do you think I should take them with all the wine I've been drinking?"

"You will be fine. I think it will steady your nerves. I'll be back in just a minute."

Within a few moments, his friend returned with several of his pills. He swallowed them with another drink of wine.

"I'm out of wine."

"No, you're not. I brought you another bottle. I think you could have one more drink and then we should try and drive out of here. I will go

18

out and take a look at the roads and then return to let you know of their condition. If they are passable, we should leave tonight. If not, one more day won't hurt. It is supposed to snow this weekend, and then winter will really set in. We will be long gone before anyone finds what is spread out all over the yard."

"You are a good friend."

"I am, aren't I? Stay put, I'll be right back."

He watched as his friend walked out of the garage. He could see him from the windows staring at him from atop the wood pile, even though the fog had begun to descend from the tree line of the mountains. He would have to go very slowly down the mountains in the dark and the smoky veil that made it even more difficult to see. He was glad his friend would be with him. He had excellent eyesight and exceptional awareness within the dark.

His friend had gray hair and yellow eyes with a sliver of black in the middle of them. The black slivers were like pendants that hung from the top of the eye and constantly expanded and contracted in size as they looked at you. But as he studied them now, he realized they were not looking at him. He began to think they never really looked at him. They only examined him.

Yes, they were forever staring at me. Just like her eyes. Her damn black eyes were always examining me too. I could even hear them judging me. I could hear them as if they had mouths; the words were so loud and distinct and always belittling me. Always. Well, she won't criticize me anymore, will she? And where the hell did that cat of hers go? Shit, those damn cat hairs are all over the car. Always shedding those fucking hairs. Even on my wine glass, god dammit.

He closed his eyes and his body slumped over in the front seat of the car. The garage was now full of exhaust fumes and with all the pills and alcohol in his body, he would never wake up. The police would rule it a suicide - murder when they found him and what remained of her severed body in the spring.

It was a gray Grimalkin, a cat often said to be associated with the devil and witchcraft. Those who had lived in that "holler" for generations, would call it an animal as old as the mountains. It was not a coincidence that he heard the cat tell him to kill her and himself. Anyone around those parts would have told him and her that you should leave it alone. After all, you can't domesticate a feral cat.

The Robber Bridegroom

Once upon a time, there was a miller who had a beautiful daughter. When she came of age he wished that she was provided for and well married. He thought, "If a respectable suitor comes and asks for her hand in marriage, I will give her to him."

Not long afterward a suitor came who appeared to be very rich, and because the miller could find no fault with him, he promised his daughter to him. The girl, however, did not like him as much as a bride should like her bridegroom. She did not trust him, and whenever she saw him or thought about him, she felt within her heart a sense of horror.

One time he said to her, "You are engaged to marry me, but you have never once paid me a visit."

The girl replied, "I don't know where your house is."

Then the bridegroom said, "My house is out in the dark woods."

Looking for an excuse, she said that she would not be able to find the way there.

The bridegroom said, "Next Sunday you must come out to me. I have already invited guests. I will make a trail of ashes so that you can find your way through the woods."

20

When Sunday came, and it was time for the girl to start on her way, she became frightened, although she herself did not know exactly why. To mark the path, she filled both her pockets full of peas and lentils. At the entrance of the forest, there was a trail of ashes, which she followed, but at every step, she threw a couple of peas to the ground, to the right, and to the left. She walked almost the whole day until she came to the middle of the woods, where it was the darkest, and there stood a solitary house. She did not like it, because it looked so dark and sinister. She went inside, but no one was there. It was totally quiet.

Suddenly a voice called out:

> Turn back, turn back, you young bride.
> You are in a murderer's house.

The girl looked up and saw that the voice came from a bird, which was hanging in a cage on the wall. It cried out again:

> Turn back, turn back, you young bride.
> You are in a murderer's house.

Then the beautiful bride went from one room to another, walking through the whole house, but it was empty, and not a human soul was to be found. Finally, she came to the cellar. A very old woman was sitting there shaking her head. "Could you tell me," said the girl, "if my bridegroom lives here?"

"Oh, you poor child," replied the old woman, "where did you come from? You are in a murderer's den. You think you are a bride soon to be married, but it is death that you will be marrying. Look, they made me put a large kettle of water on the fire. When they have captured you, they will chop you to pieces without mercy, cook you, and eat you, for they are cannibals. If I do not show you compassion and save you, you are doomed."

21

With this, the old woman led her behind a large barrel where she could not be seen. "Be quiet as a mouse," she said. "Do not make a sound or move, or all will be over with you. Tonight when the robbers are asleep we will escape. I have long waited for an opportunity."

This had scarcely happened when the godless band came home. They were dragging with them another maiden. They were drunk and paid no attention to her screams and sobs. They gave her wine to drink, three glasses full, one glass of white, one glass of red, and one glass of yellow, which caused her heart to break. Then they ripped off her fine clothes, laid her on a table, chopped her beautiful body in pieces, and sprinkled salt on it. The poor bride behind the barrel trembled and shook, for she saw well what fate the robbers had planned for her.

One of them noticed a gold ring on the murdered girl's little finger. Because it did not come off easily, he took an ax and chopped the finger off, but it flew into the air and over the barrel, falling right into the bride's lap. The robber took a light and looked for it, but could not find it.

Then another one said, "Did you look behind the large barrel?"

But the old woman cried out, "Come and eat. You can continue looking in the morning. That finger won't run away from you."

Then the robbers said, "The old woman is right." They gave up their search and sat down to eat. The old woman poured a sleeping potion into their wine so that they soon lay down in the cellar and fell asleep, snoring.

When the bride heard them snoring she came out from behind the barrel and had to step over the sleepers, for they lay all in rows on the ground. She was afraid that she might awaken one of them, but God helped her, and she got through safely. The old woman

22

went upstairs with her, opened the door, and they hurried out of the murderer's den as fast as they could.

The wind had blown away the trail of ashes, but the peas and lentils had sprouted and grown up, and showed them the way in the moonlight. They walked all night, arriving at the mill the next morning. Then the girl told her father everything, just as it had happened.

When the wedding day came, the bridegroom appeared. The miller had invited all his relatives and acquaintances. As they sat at the table, each one was asked to tell something. The bride sat still and said nothing. Then the bridegroom said to the bride, "Come, sweetheart, don't you know anything? Tell us something, like the others have done."

She answered:

"Then I will tell about a dream. I was walking alone through the woods when finally, I came to a house. Inside there was not a single human soul, but on the wall, there was a bird in a cage. It cried out:

> Turn back, turn back, you young bride.
> You are in a murderer's house.

Then it cried out the same thing again. Darling, it was only a dream. Then I went through all the rooms. They were all empty, and there was something so eerie in there. Finally, I went down into the cellar, and there sat a very old woman, shaking her head. I asked her, 'Does my bridegroom live in this house?'

"She answered, 'Alas poor child, you have gotten into a murderer's den. Your bridegroom does live here, but he intends to chop you to pieces and kill you, and then he intends to cook you and eat you.'

"Darling, it was only a dream. After that, the old woman hid me behind a large barrel. I had scarcely hidden myself there when the robbers came home, dragging a girl with them. They gave her three kinds of wine to drink: white, red, and yellow, which caused her heart to stop beating. Darling, it was only a dream. After that, they took off her fine clothes, and chopped her beautiful body to pieces on a table, then sprinkled salt on it. Darling, it was only a dream. Then one of the robbers saw that there was still a ring on her ring finger. Because it was hard to get the ring off, he took an ax and chopped off the finger. The finger flew through the air behind the large barrel and fell into my lap. And here is the finger with the ring."

With these words, she pulled out the finger and showed it to everyone who was there.

The robber, who had during this story become as white as chalk, jumped up and tried to escape, but the guests held him fast and turned him over to the courts. Then he and his whole band were executed for their shameful deeds.

An Old Beginning

O nce upon a time, there was a family who lived in Ireland but no longer took pleasure in the land where they had resided for many, many years. They despised the English monarchy that ruled over them, and they understood that their critical tone and actions would only arouse additional scrutiny and in all likelihood poverty or death, so they decided to leave. The Revolutionary War was over and they believed they could find a new home in the new nation; a nation that would allow them to escape the constant religious persecution they had endured and would welcome those who shared their opinions concerning English despots. So, they immigrated to America in 1809.

The voyage across the Atlantic lasted two months and it was July when they arrived in New York and several months later before they reached the port of Charleston. They used all of their money for the journey and when they arrived in Charleston, all they had left were two suitcases: one packed with clothes and the other filled with religious artifacts. Despite the family's objections, the father sold several of the silver relics to buy a horse and some food which enabled them to venture west and begin rebuilding their life.

They settled in the mountains of north Georgia, and though it was December and cold, the land reminded everyone of the Irish mountains from whence they came. They found a flat area surrounded by woods and a mountain stream, with views of the mountains that went on for miles. The father knew it would be difficult to build everything necessary with only his two daughters and wife to help, but his daughters were determined and strong. With his wife's blessing and encouragement, they began, and within two months the foundation for their new cabin was established.

Three Cherokee Indians watched this family from the woods each day. The warriors were impressed with the strength of the young women and captivated by the beauty of the eldest daughter. The girls both had long, thick blonde hair and eyes that were as green as the land from which they came, but the eldest daughter also had the face and body of a goddess. Her sister, though not ugly, had a simpler nature about her in body and spirit, but she was as strong as any man her age.

In March, the warriors approached the family and began to establish a relationship with them with the intent of persuading the father to allow one of them to take his eldest daughter as a wife. The father and mother knew that these strong fierce-looking men could try and take whatever they wanted, but they also believed that they would be able to overcome any adversity that befell them, so they welcomed these encounters and allowed them to continue.

The father learned that the one who seemed to be the leader of the three, was named Dan-u-wo-a, and that his two friends were named E-no-li and Mo-he. Through a series of hand gestures and sounds, the family later learned the meaning of those names and, as you would expect, the leader's name, Dan-u-wo-a, meant warrior. E-no-li was named for the black fox and Mo-he for the elk. And once learned, the family could see that those men had been well-named. At least it appeared so, but it was not true.

These men were very violent and had evil intent; men who the Cherokees said had walked with the "black spirit" and were no longer "principled people." They had been expelled from their tribe and now lived a nomadic life, taking advantage of anyone that they encountered. Dan-u-wo-a was cunning and he told his "brothers" that they should be very careful with these "white invaders" before they attacked them and made them "pay for their arrogance." His "brothers" didn't understand why, but they never questioned Dan-u-wo-a's instincts and did as he requested.

The Cherokees learned the names of the family and found it odd that their names all had the same sound to them, though it was just because they thought the last name should be pronounced each time, and though the father tried, he could not stop them from doing so. Others might struggle to pronounce the family names based upon their Celtic spellings, but the Cherokees did not because they learned the names from a verbal perspective. Thus, the braves called the father Kee-an (Cian) Dullahan, the mother Deer-dra Dullahan, (Deirdre), the eldest daughter Fee-a Dullahan (Fiadh), and the youngest daughter Nessa Dullahan.

It wasn't long before the entire family recognized that all three men wanted Fiadh as their wife. They were worried about how the men might try to resolve that desire amongst themselves and also how they would react when Fiadh told them she was not interested in becoming a wife to any of them. As Cian discussed this dilemma with both his daughters, Deirdre announced to everyone that she had a premonition about these men. She said she saw them walking among the shadow world and that they were evil.

It was at that time that Nessa revealed she had sensed someone else was watching them now each time the warriors came to visit. Cian and Deirdre had always known their youngest daughter had been blessed by the fairy folk. She not only had the ability to sense what was present within the world around her long before anyone else, but she could also move through the woods undetected. As such, Cian asked her to find out who it was she sensed out there in the woods the next time she felt the presence.

A week later, after the braves had visited and left, Nessa felt another spirit observing them and followed it. She tracked it to the edge of the mountains and saw that the entity was that of an Indian woman; a woman who had now joined two other Indian women who seemed to be waiting for her. Nessa soon heard the angry tone of their voices and was about to leave when she saw E-no-li arrive and begin arguing with one of them. Moments later, Mo-he and Dan-u-wo-a appeared and when they did, the women attacked them. Nessa watched as the warriors subdued each woman, cut their throats, and threw their dying bodies to the ground. Nessa knew exactly what those three men would do next, so she disappeared back into the woods and ran through them as if she was light itself until she was back home and told her family what she had just witnessed.

The three women who were killed that day were the wives of the three warriors and the "black spirits" that surrounded them now told the men what to do next. The warriors cut open the chest of each woman, removed the heart, and squeezed it over the women's faces. They each stuck two fingers into the blood and drew two lines on their forehead, cheeks, and chin. They were no longer concerned with who would take Fiadh as their wife. They knew that before the end of the day, each of them would have her and her sister as their slaves and that the two daughters would witness their parents burned alive. They

27

picked up the dead bodies of their wives and threw them off the mountain and ran back to the Dullahan homestead.

Cian and Deirdre were sitting on their front porch when the evil warriors drew close. They looked for Fiadh and Nessa but they didn't see either of them. Though the blood on their faces reflected their lust and their bodies wanted to race toward Cian and Deirdre, they didn't. Dan-u-wo-a held them back and told them to be alert as they walked slowly toward the porch. Dan-u-wo-a carried a knife in each hand and E-no-li and Mo-he held a bow with a notched arrow.

As they passed the perimeter fence, Nessa came out of the house and screamed. The Indians smiled at each other, thinking that their appearance prompted fear, and yelled back at Nessa. But, they had misinterpreted her loud familial calls. Nessa wasn't screaming from fear. She was screaming for her sister and before the three braves could take another step, they saw someone riding toward them on a black horse.

E-no-li and Mo-he fired an arrow at the rider and though the arrows entered the body, the rider didn't stop. The three men smelled Fiadh before they saw her and what they smelled reminded them of rotting fish. When Fiadh approached them, they were unable to move as they believed they were looking at a "black spirit." In essence, they were correct. Fiadh was indeed the rider atop the horse, but she was no longer Fiadh. She was the changeling spirit she had always been and was now holding her head of emerald isle green eyes and long flowing golden hair, with her left hand.

The attractive nature of her face was gone. In its place, was a devilish grin with a mouth full of sharp teeth. Her ears stuck out from her head like the ears of a wolf and she had long claws that extended and retracted into her hairy hands and feet like that of a large cat. Before they could do anything else, Fiadh screamed. The braves dropped their weapons and covered their ears with their hands, but they could not stop the sound from piercing their eardrums and causing them to bleed. When Fiadh screamed again, the bodies of the Indians blistered with boils which burst open exposing their bones.

One by one, she called out their names, and as she did, each Cherokee warrior fell to the ground dead. Fiadh rode up to each one and spit upon them and their bodies began to melt into the earth. She stood watch over them, spitting on them until there was nothing left but their weapons, which Nessa retrieved.

28

The Dullahan name may have been unfamiliar in the new America, but it was very familiar in the land from which they escaped. The Dullahans did leave Ireland to escape religious persecution like many others, but unlike the Catholics, the Dullahans worshipped something with a more basic essence; one borne out of the ground and the land. The Dullahans were never bothered again by Indians, though there were some unfortunate, but unscrupulous thieves that encountered a similar fate as the three evil warriors.

Early settlers in America loved stories that captured their imagination. They enjoyed the tales they read about the "monster" that roamed the woods, laughing and knowing that these "yarns" were merely made up to keep people interested in the "unknown west" of their new nation. But a man in New York thought the newspaper articles that mentioned the names of the settlers and the Indians, made the story seem more real and those images resided within his subconscious for many years.

Though it cannot be stated with any degree of certainty that Washington Irving's story of the headless horseman, written in 1820, was based upon the articles he had read years earlier about the creature that roamed the "creepy hollows of the northern mountains of Georgia," it did have a familiar similarity to objective readers who knew what they had seen. But Mr. Irving also traveled extensively in England and could have heard the stories of the Dullahan there. That monster was certainly well-known in that part of the world and was not as easily dismissed as a myth as it was in America.

Mr. Korbes

Once upon a time, there were a rooster and a hen who wanted to take a journey together. So the rooster built a handsome carriage with four red wheels and hitched four mice to it. The hen climbed aboard with the rooster, and they drove away together.

Not long afterward they met a cat, who said, "Where are you going?"

The rooster answered, "We're on our way to Mr. Korbes's house."

"Take me with you," said the cat.

The rooster answered, "Gladly. Climb on behind, so you won't fall off the front. Be careful not to get my red wheels dirty. Roll, wheels. Whistle, mice. We're on our way to Mr. Korbes's house."

Then a millstone came along, then an egg, then a duck, then a pin, and finally a needle. They all climbed aboard the carriage and rode with them.

But when they arrived at Mr. Korbes's house, he was not there. The mice pulled the carriage into the barn. The hen and the rooster flew onto a pole. The cat sat down in the fireplace and the duck in the water bucket. The egg rolled itself up in a towel. The pin stuck itself into a chair cushion. The needle jumped onto the bed in the middle of the pillow. The millstone lay down above the door.

Then Mr. Korbes came home. He went to the fireplace, wanting to make a fire, and the cat threw ashes into his face. He ran quickly into the kitchen to wash himself, and the duck splashed water into his face. He wanted to dry himself off with the towel, but the egg rolled against him, broke, and glued his eyes shut. Wanting to rest, he sat down in the chair, and the pin pricked him. He fell into a rage and threw himself onto his bed, but when he laid his head on the pillow, the needle pricked him, causing him to scream and run out of the house. As he ran through the front door the millstone jumped down and struck him dead.

Mr. Korbes must have been a very wicked man.

The Medical Technologist

O nce upon a time, there was a beautiful young girl who graduated from the University of Tennessee with a B.A. in Medical Technology. She loved working at the University of Tennessee Medical Center, where she had trained. But instead of working in the main laboratory, she desired a job in the research department which was overseen by her organic chemistry instructor from the university. She believed he was one of those teachers who was responsible for helping her find her true "calling." His name was Dr. Alpiner.

Dr. Alpiner had helped Elisa find her way in college, but it was her mother who made college possible. Her mother had raised Elisa on her own since she was just two years old after her husband left her for another woman. Lisa, at that time, was still in college, a year away from getting her nursing degree, but with court-ordered child support and help from her friends, she was able to work and continue school while still caring for her beloved Elisa.

When she wasn't at work or in class, Lisa spent all her time with her young child. She only slept a few hours a day because of her clinical rotations and work demands, but no matter how tired she felt, her body renewed itself once she was with her daughter. Elisa loved her mother dearly and she excelled in every aspect of life with Lisa's guidance. Lisa wanted her daughter to grow up to be a strong and independent woman and she did everything possible to ensure she had the physical as well as the educational tools she needed to do so.

Lisa taught Elisa to swim and read her at least three books a day. Elisa thrived in that environment and by the time she was five, she was as fast as children twice her age within the pool and she could read at a third-grade level. She was beating high school swimmers and winning swimming tournaments by the time she was eight, and studying advanced math principles and reading at a high school level. And though she liked reading any book that her mother gave her, her favorites were "The Narnia Chronicles" by C.S. Lewis, and "The Hobbit" and "The Lord of the Rings" trilogy by J.R.R. Tolkien. Those stories never got old for her and she returned to them whenever she wanted to escape to those worlds for a moment, which she did frequently, especially after she turned nine.

On her ninth birthday, her mother took her to eat at her favorite Italian restaurant where they had their favorite calzones. After dinner, they saw an extended version of "The Return of the King" at her favorite movie theater which had large reclining chairs. They enjoyed a birthday dessert of large chocolate and vanilla ice cream cones while they watched the movie. Afterward, Lisa told her daughter she had one more surprise for her as they walked downtown. Lisa could tell they were headed to her favorite book store, but she acted like she wasn't sure what her mother was doing.

Unfortunately, they didn't make it to the book store that evening. As they passed a dark alley, a man jumped out and pulled her mother into it. Elisa reached out to help her mother but he knocked her back and her head hit the pavement so hard that she lost consciousness. She woke up in the hospital the next morning and saw her mother's friend beside her bed and immediately asked about her mother. The friend couldn't answer the question at first. She leaned over and grabbed Elisa's hand as she began to cry. Elisa screamed at her, demanding to know about her mother, and finally heard the words she feared. Her mother was dead.

Elisa closed her eyes and silently saw her mother in her mind as if she was watching a movie. She saw her getting her degree, reading to her every day, encouraging her at thousands of swimming lessons, helping her with her schoolwork, their walks in the park and trips to the zoo, the weekends they spent at movie theaters, and all of the special cookouts and celebrations. Everything that they had ever done together was there in her mind and she played that movie over and over, unresponsive to anyone else in the room for twenty-four hours.

The next day, the child psychologist encouraged Elisa to open her eyes and talk to them and she did. And though everyone thought the child psychologist had said all the right words, it wasn't her words that prompted Elisa to begin communicating. She was just ready to do so. When the hospital and social services contacted her father, he said he was sorry but he never even came by to see his daughter. Carolyn, her

33

mother's friend, received approval as a foster mother. Elisa was happy to go home with someone that she and her mother liked and she agreed to see a counselor as long as it was deemed necessary.

Six months later, the counselor determined that Elisa had adjusted well to her new reality and with the girl's approval, Carolyn and her husband began the formal adoption process. Her father did not object and within another six months, Elisa became Carolyn and Jim's daughter. From all appearances, one would think Elisa had moved on from her mother's death and was doing well in her new situation. But therapy had only taught Elisa that it was easier to project an outward appearance of composure and to conceal the feelings of anger that continued to circulate within her body like proteins in her blood.

Medication prescribed by the counselors helped. Winning also helped. The medication controlled the desire to lash out at her peers who appeared to have a perfect life. Winning allowed her to focus her mind and channel her anger into stamina, strength, and speed in the swimming pool, and prevented her from beating the shit out of her classmates or anyone who pissed her off. She was very good at channeling all of that negative energy into positive outcomes. And she won. She won so often, that it not only enabled her to receive a scholarship to college but also, more importantly, prevented people from questioning her about how she felt. To them, she was just a driven athlete, and to some extent that was true. But the anger and sense of loss were always present. And then she met Dr. Alpiner.

She realized she was simply going through the motions in college until she heard his first lecture. The attraction was immediate. At least on her part. It took some time before Dr. Alpiner realized how enamored the bright, beautiful, young athlete was with him. Though he took that as a compliment, he knew professor-student relationships would end up very badly for him, especially considering he was married and a well-known tenured instructor. Plus, he had been warned by the university that it couldn't happen again. Neither they nor his wife would put up with an embarrassing third time. But he could tell she was bright and silently asking for his guidance, so he agreed to serve as her mentor through school.

Within a year, she became a lab assistant for him in his research department at the University of Tennessee Medical Center. He was conducting research on smoking cessation, with the theory that he could develop a pill that would stop smoking from the first day it was taken. It was in that environment, that Elisa realized that she loved the laboratory discipline. The methodical processes required to achieve an outcome reminded her of the hours she spent training to succeed in swimming. Working alongside Dr. Alpiner was also a strong motivator and, with his help, she was accepted into the medical technology program and graduated with honors.

Soon after she graduated, a permanent full-time medical technologist position became available in his lab. She accepted the job and was given the title of Chief Technologist, Metabolic Chemistry Research Department. She loved the title and welcomed the sexual episodes that occurred in the laboratory with Dr. Alpiner. He wasn't worried now that she was no longer a student. He knew she wouldn't tell his wife because she was too captivated by his knowledge and his sexual prowess as evidenced by her apparent insatiable appetites.

They sometimes even stayed overnight in his laboratory office, sleeping on the leather sofa until early morning. Just before he left, they would have an adventuresome encounter of some sort, but he soon began to sense he was getting older. His joints were starting to ache from all the positions they tried. But "arthritis be damned" he always told himself when he saw Elisa again.

About six months later, he noticed that he was not only having pain in his joints, but his testicles were also hurting and he told Elisa that they needed to forgo their physical relationship for a while. Though Elisa was disappointed, she said she understood. It was several weeks later that he dropped the beaker on the floor and grabbed his eyes as he screamed out loud. She asked him what was wrong and he said he saw something crawling within the inside of his eyes and it felt like a hot poker had been stuck into them.

"Oh, that's just the Loa Loa adult worm. I injected you with the microfilariae almost a year ago. The microfilariae are causing the joint pain and inflammation and the aching in your testicles. If I were to squeeze them right now, I bet you would almost pass out from the pain."

"What are you talking about - how?"

"The research assistant on the third floor is studying parasitic infections and cures and she was more than willing to help me once she knew what you had done. Now that you have adult worms, you are going to need an antibiotic. Ivermectin is what my lab assistant friend recommends. That adult worm that is in your conjunctiva can be

35

surgically removed if you want, but it has to be paralyzed with a topical anesthetic and if not done correctly, will just slither away. And I don't think you want all that attention, do you?"

"Why?"

"Because you shouldn't be cheating on your wife, the mother of your four children. Granted they are grown and in high school, but still, it's not right. Do you want to start the Ivermectin? I have some."

"Yes, yes. Start it. I can't stand this pain."

"You will have to stay here through the night, as you will need another dose in 12 hours. Otherwise..."

"No, no, that's fine. Just do it!"

Elisa injected Dr. Alpiner with the Ivermectin and in just a few hours, he became mute and incontinent and found it difficult to move.

"Damn, the lab assistant said that might happen with a disproportionate amount of medicine," Elisa said as she winked and gave him another injection. "This next shot will probably induce a coma from encephalopathy and then in all likelihood, you will die. Well, not probably. It's more of a certainty. And it will look like you had a stroke and I will agree that's what it looked like to me. I'll be distraught and crying, of course.

"Unfortunately, I will have to tell them we were having sex when you complained of your head hurting and fell over, but that's just so they don't go looking any further. And they won't, considering that everyone knows of your past. I do wonder, besides the students you assaulted, how many other women did you rape? I should have asked you that before you became mute, but you could write it down for me. But no, what am I thinking? You would just lie and, believe me, I know a liar when I see one.

"What's that you are saying with your eyes? You're sorry? I know, I know. I will probably be asked to leave, but that's okay. I'm ready to move on.

"I just wish my mother was here to see you in this pathetic state. You do remember my mother, don't you? The one you assaulted and murdered in the alley off State Street, fourteen years ago? The one who had her little nine-year-old daughter with her. I thought it was anger that motivated me all my life until I heard your voice and then I knew it was more than just anger. It was revenge.

"That voice in the lecture hall. It awoke something inside of me and made me remember. You didn't realize it, but I wasn't immediately unconscious when you knocked my mother to the ground. I heard you bragging about what you were going to do to her before I blacked out. Disgusting. It's amazing how your brain has this ability to recall what you had locked away in the deep dark recesses of your mind. You know, in that 'forgotten forever file drawer.'

"Only the information is not gone. Like an erased hard drive; the information is still there and still retrievable. You just have to know how to get to it, and in this case, all it took was your voice. It triggered the awareness and made me go into that dark room and open the drawer. And when I did, I remembered what I had tried to forget.

"It's also quite remarkable that your brain allows you to do things you had no idea you could do. I abhorred having sex with you, but it was just another exercise for me. And I've been used to mind-numbing exercise my entire life. You can't succeed in swimming unless you can overcome the physical exhaustion your body endures with a strong will. I wasn't ever really there with you. I was back in the pool, just waiting for today. But you did give me a lot of pleasure during the past year. I could see it in your face as the pain began to spread through your body and I so enjoyed that. And then when you dropped the beaker and screamed, I was so happy I almost screamed along with you, because I knew the end was near and I'd soon be able to stop swimming."

Frau Trude

Once upon a time, there was a small girl who was strong-willed and forward, and whenever her parents said anything to her, she disobeyed them. How could anything go well with her?

One day she said to her parents, "I have heard so much about Frau Trude. Someday I want to go to her place. People say such amazing things are seen there, and such strange things happen there, that I have become very curious.

Her parents strictly forbade her, saying, "Frau Trude is a wicked woman who commits godless acts. If you go there, you will no longer be our child."

But the girl paid no attention to her parents and went to Frau Trude's place anyway. When she arrived there, Frau Trude asked, "Why are you so pale?"

"Oh," she answered, trembling all over, "I saw something that frightened me."

"What did you see?"

"I saw a black man on your steps."

"That was a charcoal burner."

"Then I saw a green man."

"That was a huntsman."

"Then I saw a blood-red man."

"That was a butcher."

"Oh, Frau Trude, it frightened me when I looked through your window and could not see you, but instead saw the devil with a head of fire."

"Aha!" she said. "So you saw the witch properly outfitted. I have been waiting for you and wanting you for a long time. Light the way for me now!"

With that, she turned the girl into a block of wood and threw it into the fire. When it was thoroughly aglow she sat down next to it, and warmed herself by it, saying, "It gives such a bright light!

True Blue

Once upon a time, she was considered the most beautiful woman in the world. She was the world's most famous fashion model, and her face and figure could be identified by those even in remote parts of the world because she modeled something that everyone could identify with: blue jeans. That was it. Just blue jeans. Not make-up of any kind. No magical herbal supplement that she took every day to maintain her perfect skin and figure. No specific diet or one of the gazillion types of drinks that came and went like drops of rain. No, she was only known for one thing and that was blue jeans.

Now, granted, these were very good-looking blue jeans. Both men and women were impressed and complimentary of the way she looked in those denim extensions of her body. And the photographers who took her pictures for the advertisements were very shrewd. They recognized her type of natural beauty didn't come along often. She wasn't completely unique in that regard. There were other women whose beauty had influenced society and even history. But even so, no other woman at that particular time was deemed as beautiful as "True Blue."

That was her name, or what everyone called her because it was the brand of the jeans she wore. No one knew her actual name and no one really cared. If she was seen in public, her fans shouted, "True Blue!" and she waved at them. The media shouted, "True Blue, over here!" and she turned to them and posed as they took her picture. Those in the media who thought they would concentrate solely on her face found that those pictures were seldom used. No. Everyone knew that the "money shot" was her, all of her, in her unmistakable blue jeans.

Over time she began to understand what she did had very little meaning, even though she seemed uninterested in trying to correct that belief. That's because she couldn't. The memories of her past were very debilitating and she couldn't allow them to control her like they did before she became famous. Her mother died in a psychiatric unit when she was a child. Her father, unable to look at her without seeing the woman he married, left her to be raised by foster care and she never saw him again. She kept those memories sealed in her past, but no one can live in the present without acknowledging the past at some point in their life. Many have tried but no one is successful forever.

The images of the past were subtle at first, a misinterpreted shadow that disappeared into the forest of photographers became a face that looked very familiar, only to be lost amongst all the flashing lights. Visions of the different shades of red in an autumn forest in the hair of a young fan reminded her of how her hair had once been described. She saw that same hair again a week later, only this time she also saw the eyes of the person. Within those eyes were irises the color of antique copper brown, much like her own, even though she had been told that shade was extremely rare.

And then she saw the face. The face that looked like her own and appeared to have been chiseled by a masterful artisan. The nose, lips, eyebrows, chin; each feature was in perfect harmony and complemented her hair and eyes. The skin that covered her entire upper body, which was very feminine and athletic at the same time, was unblemished and a perfect shade of tan. That's when she realized she was looking in the mirror again, wondering why she had been placed in this room. She didn't like this room or this building.

There were no photographers in here. No celebrities. She wasn't sure where or when they left but they were there one day and then they were gone, replaced with people who only wore white. The same drab white clothes every day. It was disgusting. And these people were mean and told her to do things she didn't like and said things that didn't make any sense.

She was angry too. They tried to make her wear pants but she was not going to cover up her lower body and legs which were tattooed to look like she was wearing the perfect blue jeans. The subtle but distinct tones of dark and faded blues in all the right places. The stitched crease that looked like it went up both sides of her legs. The straight-line stitched pockets on her voluptuous firm curves in the back. The pockets on her thighs with the metal stud on the top of the pocket and a curved stitched opening that disappeared just below one

41

of the belt loops. And the belt loops that appeared three-dimensional if someone examined them closely, but like her jeans, were only colored ink.

She was mad that they had surgically removed the zipper but she wouldn't let that stop her from replacing it. She had already begun acquiring the necessary materials from one of the men who worked there that she allowed to come into her room and do things with her. She would kill him too, just like the other one, as soon she had everything she needed. *The people in here are so stupid. They never learn. They cannot wear True Blue jeans. Only I can.*

The Three Feathers

Once upon a time, there was a king who had three sons, two of whom were clever and intelligent, but the third one did not talk very much, was simple-minded, and the only name they gave him was *the Simpleton.*

When the king became old and weak and thought that he was nearing his end, he did not know which of his sons should inherit the kingdom after him, so he said to them, "Go forth, and the one of you who brings me the finest carpet, he shall be king after my death."

So there would be no dispute among them, he led them to the front of his castle, blew three feathers into the air, and said, "As they fly, so shall you go."

The one feather flew to the east, the other to the west, and the third feather flew straight ahead, falling quickly to the ground after going only a short distance. The one brother went to the right, the other to the left, and they laughed at the Simpleton who had to stand there where the third feather had fallen.

The Simpleton sat down and was sad. Then he suddenly noticed that there was a trapdoor next to his feather. He lifted it up, found a stairway, and climbed down inside. He came to another door and knocked on it, upon which he heard someone calling out from within:

"Maiden green and small,
Hopping toad,
Hopping toad's puppy,

43

Hop to and fro,
Quickly see who is outside."

The door opened, and he saw a big, fat toad sitting there, surrounded by a large number of little toads. The fat toad asked what he wanted.

The Simpleton answered, "I would like the most beautiful and finest carpet."

Then the fat toad called to a young toad, saying:

"Maiden green and small,
Hopping toad,
Hopping toad's puppy,
Hop to and fro,
Bring me the large box."

The young toad brought the box, and the fat toad opened it, then gave the Simpleton a carpet from it. It was so beautiful and so fine, the like of which could never have been woven in the world above. He thanked the toad and climbed back out.

Now the other two thought that their brother was so stupid that he would not find anything to bring home. "Why should we spend a lot of effort looking for a carpet?" they said, so they took some pieces of coarse cloth from the first shepherd's wife they came to and took these back home to the king.

At the same time they returned home, the Simpleton arrived, bringing his beautiful carpet. When the king saw it, he was astounded, and said, "It is only right that the kingdom should go to my youngest son."

However, the two other sons gave their father no peace, saying that it would be impossible for the Simpleton to become king because he lacked understanding in all things. They asked him to declare another contest. Then the father said, "He who brings me the most beautiful ring shall inherit the kingdom." Leading the three brothers outside, he blew the three feathers into the air that they were to follow.

The two oldest brothers again went to the east and to the west, and the Simpleton's feather again flew straight ahead, falling down next to the door in the ground. Once again, he climbed down to the fat toad and told it that he needed the most beautiful ring. The toad had the box brought out again and gave him from it a ring that glistened with precious stones and was so beautiful that no goldsmith on earth could have made it.

The two oldest brothers laughed at the Simpleton, who was going to look for a golden ring, and they took no effort at all. Instead, they drove the nails out of an old wagon ring and brought it to the king. However, when the Simpleton presented his ring, the king said once again, "The kingdom belongs to him."

The two oldest sons tormented the king endlessly, until finally, he declared a third contest, saying that he who would bring home the most beautiful woman should have the kingdom. Once again he blew the three feathers into the air and they flew in the same directions as before.

Without hesitating, the Simpleton went back to the fat toad and said, "I am supposed to take home the most beautiful woman."

"Oh!" answered the toad. "The most beautiful woman! She is not here at the moment, but you shall have her nonetheless."

The fat toad gave him a hollowed-out yellow turnip, to which were harnessed six little mice.

The Simpleton said sadly, "What am I to do with this?"

The toad answered, "Just put one of my little toads inside it."

Then he grabbed one of them from the group and set it inside the yellow coach. The little toad was scarcely inside when it turned into a beautiful young lady, the turnip into a coach, and the six mice into horses. He kissed her, raced away with the horses, and brought her to the king.

His brothers came along afterward. They had given no effort to find a beautiful woman, but simply brought along the first peasant women they had come upon.

After looking at them, the king said, "After my death, the kingdom belongs to my youngest son."

However, the two oldest sons again deafened the king's ears with the cry, "We cannot allow the Simpleton to become king," and they demanded that the preference should go to the brother whose woman could jump through a hoop that was hanging in the middle of the hall. They thought, "The peasant women will be able to do that very well. They are very strong, but the dainty lady will jump herself to death."

The old king gave in to this as well. The two peasant women did indeed jump through the hoop, but they were so plump that each one fell, breaking her thick arms and legs. Then the beautiful lady, that the Simpleton had brought home, jumped, and she jumped through the hoop as lightly as a deer.

After this, all the protests had to stop. Thus, the Simpleton received the crown, and he ruled wisely for a long time.

The Goombah

Once upon a time, there was a very rich father who had three sons. The father was dying and wanted to be certain that he left his company to the son who could ensure the business would endure long after he was gone. He did not know how to do that, however, because he had a very unique organization. Many members of the community, especially those in law enforcement, would suggest that the father's enterprise was built upon theft, drugs, gambling, and murder. The community and those in law enforcement were both correct in their assertions.

The father was very wise and very lucky. He easily anticipated his competition and had consistently been able to outmaneuver them over the years. It was one reason that he had lived long enough for cancer to become the cause of his death and not several projectiles, traveling at 2600 feet per second, that had been fired at his head.

The father often sat up at night and stared out the bulletproof window of his bedroom, but he was never alone in those dark, early morning hours. His wife had died some time ago, also from cancer and his thoughts and memories kept him company as he dwelled on both for many weeks. He remembered how his oldest son was so daring and unafraid. He laughed when he saw him get bitten by bugs or snakes that didn't like the way he examined them and he saw how those bugs or snakes came to regret their impulsive nature.

He remembered how his second-oldest son could convince his older brother to do or try anything. He could hear his wife telling him, "That boy will be trouble when he gets older," provided he didn't end up getting his brother killed. And he and his wife would laugh about all the times they had cautioned the oldest son to think before he did something his younger brother told him to do and had instructed the younger brother to stop getting his older sibling into trouble.

And then his thoughts turned to his youngest son. He was funny and liked to read, especially Shakespeare. He didn't care that his older brothers teased him about the books he read. He ignored them and his father thought that showed a great deal of strength. He laughed when his young son told him it didn't take strength to ignore a "bunch of idiots," and then pronounce with a poised voice some quote from Shakespeare, one of his favorites being: "Lord, what fools these mortals be!" from the play "A Midsummer Night's Dream."

"Ah, Maria, what am I to do?" the father would ask in a whispered voice every night and wait for an answer from the shadows within the room, but one never came. Without spiritual guidance from Maria and on the third week of his late-night deliberations, he devised a plan that would help him decide to whom he would hand over the reins of the business. He knew his oldest son would be unhappy with the decision, considering that he would believe it should automatically go to him, based upon their cultural traditions. But he was prepared for that and knew how to deal with that issue.

Before he announced the plan to all three sons, he brought his oldest son into his bedroom and talked with him about his mother and all the good times that they had shared when he was younger. He then said he had a secret to tell him; one that he had never told anyone else. He told him one of the last things his mother shared before she passed away was her wish to allow each of their three sons an opportunity to succeed him before he died. He understood his oldest son could not go against the dying wishes of his mother and, just as he reasoned, the son thanked his father for sharing that secret with him and agreed to do whatever his father asked.

The father thanked his eldest son for his wisdom and loyalty and said he would talk to his brothers the next day. At dinner the next evening, he told all his sons that he was dying and that he wanted to ensure that everything he had worked for all his life would continue to prosper after he was gone. The company needed a strong and smart leader and for him to know which of his three sons should fulfill that role, he would ask that they complete two tasks.

Before he could further explain, the middle son asked his father why he was dying.

"Some form of rare cancer is all I know," he replied, awash with anger. He was used to knowing the answers that he wanted and the fact that he didn't know the reason pissed him off. But just as quickly, his cross tone dissipated and was replaced with the words of a man who had moved on toward acceptance. "But what are you going to do?" he asked as he shrugged his shoulders and began to explain what he wished from his sons.

Their first duty, he said, was for each of them to bring him the most money that they could get within twenty-four hours. He gave them no other instructions and told them they had until the next day at 5 p.m. The brothers looked at each other and the two eldest smiled because they knew this would be an easy task for them. The youngest brother simply looked at his father and said he was sorry that all of this had occurred and his father smiled and nodded his head toward him. He then stood up and said he was tired and went to bed.

The next evening at 5 p.m., the father walked into the dining room and found his three sons at the table. The eldest immediately spoke up and told his father that he had brought him a little over half a million dollars.

"How much over half a million?" his father asked.

"A thousand or ten thousand, not sure. I didn't bother to count every dollar because I'm sure I brought you the most," he announced smugly and arrogantly.

"You should have counted it," the middle son said. "I brought you $679,000, Papa."

"Bravo!" his father exclaimed. The elder brother said, "Damn," and they all laughed before they turned toward the youngest son.

"Father, my brothers brought you a lot of money but at great risk. My oldest brother robbed a cartel of their money and they will seek retribution. Sure, we will eventually overcome it, but many lives will be lost because many lives were lost in obtaining that money. My other brother robbed a bank to get his money. That theft is all over the news and now the FBI is very interested in who could have been smart and daring enough to commit such a crime. They will come here and ask questions and that is never good. I brought you this, Papa," and upon saying that he handed his father a penny.

His brothers laughed until they heard his brother speaking again.

"That is a 1943-S bronze penny. They were not supposed to use bronze for pennies during World War II, because they needed it for the war effort, but a few were made in error before they caught the mistake. That one you have is worth a little over a million dollars. No one was hurt in obtaining that coin and it was not stolen. I purchased

49

it some time ago from someone who needed money fast and was willing to make concessions that I don't think he would have made otherwise. But his bad luck was my good fortune. I think it was a good $100,000 investment, don't you?"

I am not surprised, his father thought and thanked each of his sons for completing the first task and then said that he had one more mission for them. He directed them to bring him his biggest threat. Before any questions could be asked, he said he would see them tomorrow night at exactly 5 p.m., and then the decision would be made.

Both of the older brothers told their younger sibling that he may have won the first round but they were certain he would not succeed with this assignment because he was too weak. The youngest brother said they were probably right as he watched them walk away and left him sitting at the table by himself. "Be all my sins remember'd," he whispered and then smiled as he pulled out his Shakespeare anthology and began to read.

The next night, when the father came to the table, he saw his two oldest sons holding the leaders of their largest and most dangerous competition next to them. His youngest son sat at the table with nothing but a bottle of wine. The youngest brother saluted his siblings and poured them all a glass of wine as he congratulated them for winning. The brothers toasted each other and drank the wine while the youngest brother began to speak.

"I know you don't think I brought anything to the table this time, Papa, but I did. The most dangerous threat to your organization is my two brothers. They have brought your biggest enemies here, thinking that you would have them killed, but they failed to ask themselves in doing so, why was it so easy to get these men here? The fact is, it is never that easy. These men that you see here are protected much like you and if you do anything to them, it will create a war that I'm not sure anyone will survive."

His brothers yelled at their younger brother but their father stopped them from saying anything else and asked the youngest son to continue.

"My brothers, did you not wonder why these men's bodyguards were not present when you went into their house? It is because they lost their heads earlier in the evening," the younger brother said as he bent down and pulled a sack from beneath the table. He held it over the table and allowed the heads to fall out. They made a squishing sound as they bounced against each other like overripe cantaloupes until they rested, staring at the wall and the ceiling. The older brothers immediately threw up. The father as well as the two older men were surprised by their sickness, considering everything that they knew those brothers had done and seen in the past.

"My brothers are not sick because they are horrified by what they see but because of the poison that is killing them. It was in the wine and I suspect they will be dead within another ten seconds."

The youngest son looked at his watch and counted off the seconds and at the end of ten, both of his older brothers indeed fell over dead.

"Now, Papa, if you will allow me to continue, I think we should let these men leave. They have suffered enough and they know that if necessary, I can revisit them anytime. But I don't think that will be needed because the biggest threats to your organization are gone and your enemies are now our friends."

The two men said the youngest son spoke the truth and the father rose from his chair, shook their hands, and told them they could leave. The father looked into the face of his youngest son and put his hands on his shoulders.

"Your mother would not be happy with what you have done," the father said.

"I disagree. But then, you don't remember, do you?"

With those words, the old man saw the image in his eyes. Two adolescents, one of them pointing their father's handgun at the housemaid, while the other one told her that she would have sex with both of them, or she would die. He then saw them fighting and heard the gun go off and the young woman fall to the floor. And then he heard the baby cry. The housemaid's baby that he adopted that day, hoping that would provide him atonement for what his sons had done.

"Ahhh... I see you remember now. Your wife told me everything, just before she died," he said as the old man slumped over and was caught in his adopted son's arms. He helped the old man down onto the floor, and whispered into his ear, "By the way, you did not die from cancer," as he retrieved the penny from the pocket of the old man's sweater and walked away.

51

The Spirit in the Bottle

O nce upon a time, there was a poor woodcutter who worked from morning until late at night. When he had finally saved up some money he said to his boy, "You are my only child. I want to spend the money that I have earned by the sweat of my brow on your education. Learn an honest trade so you can support me in my old age when my limbs have grown stiff and I have to sit at home."

Then the boy went to a university and studied diligently. His teachers praised him, and he remained there for some time. After he had worked through a few classes but was still not perfect in everything, the little pittance that the father had saved was all spent, and the boy had to return home to him.

"Oh," said the father sadly, "I cannot give you anything more, and in these hard times I cannot earn a heller more than what we need for our daily bread."

"Father, dear," answered the son, "don't worry about it. If it is God's will everything will turn out well for me. I will do all right."

When the father said he was going into the woods and earn some money by cutting cordwood, the son said, "I will go with you and help you."

"No, my son," said the father, "you will find it too difficult. You are not used to hard work, and will not be able to do it.

52

Furthermore, I have only one ax and no money left to buy another one with."

"Just go to the neighbor," answered the son. "He will lend you his ax until I have earned enough to buy one for myself."

So the father borrowed an ax from the neighbor, and the next morning at daybreak they went out into the woods together. The son helped his father and was quite cheerful and full of energy. When the sun was directly above them, the father said, "Let us rest now and eat our noon meal. Then all will go twice as well."

The son picked up his bread and said, "Just you rest, father. I am not tired. I will walk about a little in the woods and look for birds' nests."

"Oh, you fool," said the father, "why do you want to run about? Afterwards you will be tired and no longer able to lift an arm. Stay here, and sit down beside me."

But the son went into the woods, ate his bread, was very cheerful, and looked into the green branches to see if he could find a bird's nest. He walked to and fro until at last, he came to an enormous oak that was certainly many hundred years old, and that five men would not have been able to span. He stood there looking at it, and thought, "Many a bird must have built its nest in that tree."

Then suddenly he thought that he heard a voice. Listening, he became aware of someone calling out with a muffled voice, "Let me out. Let me out."

He looked around but could not see anything. Then he thought that the voice was coming out of the ground, so he shouted, "Where are you?"

The voice answered, "I am stuck down here among the oak roots. Let me out. Let me out."

The student began to scrape about beneath the tree, searching among the roots, until at last, he found a glass bottle in a little opening. Lifting it up, he held it against the light and then saw something shaped like a frog jumping up and down inside.

"Let me out. Let me out," it cried again, and the student, thinking no evil, pulled the cork from the bottle. Immediately a spirit ascended from it and began to grow. It grew so fast that within a few moments a horrible fellow, half as big as the tree, was standing there before the student.

"Do you know," he cried in a terrifying voice, "what your reward is for having let me out?"

"No," replied the student fearlessly. "How should I know that?"

"Then I will tell you," shouted the spirit. "I must break your neck for it."

"You should have said so sooner," answered the student, "for then I would have left you shut up inside. However, my head is going to stay where it is until more people have been consulted."

"More people here, more people there," shouted the spirit. "You shall have the reward you have earned. Do you think that I was shut up there for such a long time as a favor? No, it was a punishment. I am the mighty Mercurius. I must break the neck of whomsoever releases me."

"Calm down," answered the student. "Not so fast. First, I must know that you really were shut up in that little bottle and that you are the right spirit. If you can indeed get inside again, then I will believe it, and you may do with me whatsoever you want."

The spirit said arrogantly, "that is an easy trick," pulling himself in and making himself as thin and short as he had been before. He then crept back into the opening and through the neck of the bottle. He was scarcely inside when the student pushed the cork back into the bottle and threw it back where it had been among the oak roots. And thus, the spirit was deceived.

The student was about to return to his father, but the spirit cried out pitifully, "Oh, do let me out. Oh, do let me out."

"No," answered the student, "not a second time. I will not release a person who once tried to kill me, now that I have captured him again."

"If you will set me free," cried the spirit, "I will give you so much that you will have enough for all the days of your life."

"No," answered the student, "you would cheat me like you tried to the first time."

"You are giving away your own good fortune," said the spirit. "I will not harm you, but instead will reward you richly."

The student thought, "I will venture it. Perhaps he will keep his word, and in any event, he will not get the better of me."

So he pulled out the cork, and the spirit rose up from the bottle as before, and extended himself, becoming as large as a giant.

"Now you shall have your reward," he said, handing the student a little rag that looked just like a small bandage. He said, "If you rub a wound with the one end, it will heal, and if you rub steel or iron with the other end, it will turn into silver."

"I have to try that," said the student. He went to a tree, scratched the bark with his ax, then rubbed it with the one end of the bandage. It immediately closed together and was healed.

"Now it is all right," he said to the spirit, "and we can part."

The spirit thanked him for having freed him, and the student thanked the spirit for the present and returned to his father.

"Where have you been running about?" said the father. "Why have you forgotten your work? I said that you wouldn't get anything done."

"Don't be concerned, father. I will make it up."

"Make it up indeed," said the father angrily. "Don't bother."

"Just watch, father. I will soon cut down that tree there and make it crash."

Then he took his bandage, rubbed the ax with it, and struck a mighty blow, but because the iron had turned into silver, the cutting edge bent back on itself.

"Hey, father, just look what a bad ax you've given me. It is all bent out of shape."

The father was shocked and said, "Oh, what have you done! Now I'll have to pay for the ax, and I don't know what with. That is all the good I have from your work."

"Don't get angry," said the son, "I will pay for the ax."

"Oh, you blockhead," cried the father, "How will you pay for it? You have nothing but what I give you. You have students' tricks stuck in your head, but you don't know anything about chopping wood."

After a little while the student said, "Father, I can't work any longer after all. Let's quit for the day."

"Now then," he answered, "do you think I can stand around with my hands in my pockets like you? I have to go on working, but you may head for home."

"Father, I am here in these woods for the first time. I don't know my way alone. Please go with me."

His anger had now subsided, so the father at last let himself be talked into going home with him.

There he said to the son, "Go and sell the damaged ax and see what you can get for it. I will have to earn the difference, in order to pay the neighbor."

The son picked up the ax and took it into town to a goldsmith, who tested it, weighed it, and then said, "It is worth four hundred talers. I do not have that much cash with me."

The student said, "Give me what you have. I will lend you the rest."

The goldsmith gave him three hundred talers and owed him one hundred. Then the student went home and said, "Father, I have some money. Go and ask the neighbor what he wants for the ax."

"I already know," answered the old man. "One taler, six groschens."

"Then give him two talers, twelve groschens. That is double its worth and is plenty. See, I have more than enough money." Then

57

he gave the father a hundred talers, saying, "You shall never need anything. Live just like you want to."

"My goodness," said the old man. "Where did you get all that money?"

Then the son told him everything that had happened, and how by trusting in his luck he had made such a catch. With the money that was left, he went back to the university and continued his studies, and because he could heal all wounds with his bandage he became the most famous doctor in the whole world.

The Garage

Once upon a time, it was very hot in Augusta, Georgia. It was August so saying it was hot is like saying the day was bright and the night was dark. There had been two weeks straight of over 100-degree temperatures, with weather predictions that this pattern would continue through the end of the month. People avoided going outside and even shunned their pools because the water was more tepid than refreshing.

Those whose jobs required them to work outside only worked during the morning hours for there was no way to keep them safe as the temperatures rose throughout the afternoon. Trying to stay hydrated while working with asphalt repairing roads or in the construction or landscaping industries was almost impossible during these days, and already several men and women had died from heat strokes.

Henry was glad to be working from home that summer. Actually, Henry was always glad that he worked at home. He did not feel comfortable in large crowds and he enjoyed the solitary lifestyle he had created. He lived out in the far western part of the city, where he enjoyed the isolation of the country, but still benefited from the technology provided to residents in the urban community. During that summer, he only left the house to go to the grocery store.

He was unpacking his car in the garage after one of those trips when he dropped a jar of pickles that shattered as it hit the floor. Bending over to pick up the glass, he noticed something moving out of the corner of his eye.

The movement was in the corner of the garage; a place where his yard tools were stacked up beside the old ceramic and plastic pots he frequently used for flowers and transplanting shrubs and trees. He stopped and stared into that corner for several minutes and upon seeing nothing else, he continued picking up the glass and putting it into a garbage bag. Suddenly, he heard a rustle in that same area and when he turned to look again, he jerked his hand and a small piece of glass became embedded in his palm. He didn't believe the cut would require stitches, but it still bled a great deal and it made him mad when the blood dripped onto his new pants.

He cursed, pulled the glass out, and placed a paper towel around the wound as he hurriedly swept up the remaining pieces of glass. When he threw the plastic bag into the trash can he thought he saw a twisted shadow move again in that same dark corner of the garage and ran inside the house. He leaned up against the closed door to the garage and quietly said, "Shit." He was certain that he knew what that image was. He had seen it move twice and heard it. It was a snake, looking for a cool place within the darkness of his garage.

Henry abhorred snakes. It was the only thing he disliked about the location of his house. Out there in the woods, there were lots of ponds, and with woods and ponds in the south, came snakes. And now there was one in his garage. "Shit!" he yelled and then noticed the red drops on the kitchen floor. He looked down at his hand and the cut that he thought was minor, looked much bigger now and was dripping blood onto the floor and his pants.

He held his hand under the water of the kitchen sink and cleaned the wound. It was deeper than he had originally thought but he still didn't think it required stitches. "No, it doesn't need stitches," he told himself several times as he put pressure on the wound with a paper towel and retrieved antibacterial ointment and a Band-Aid from the bathroom. "No, it doesn't need stitches," he repeated because he knew he would have to go into the garage to get in his car in order to get to a medical facility, and "it" would be there.

He applied the ointment and Band-Aid and held it tightly against his hand for several minutes while he held it straight up into the air. After a few moments of doing this, the cut seemed stable and he went back to the kitchen to clean up the blood that had dripped onto the floor. As he mopped, the Band-Aid began to redden and he realized he would have to put something stronger on the wound.

He applied a pressure bandage with gauze and some medical tape and he felt much better about his injury. "It's just because of the location, there in the middle of my hand. That's what's causing it to bleed," he told himself and he let out a deep sigh knowing that he would not have to go out into the garage anytime soon.

60

After taking several Tylenol, he began to work on his computer, but he soon recognized that typing aggravated his hurt hand, so he stopped and decided he would just spend the day reading. He loved reading horror books and had purchased a collection of short stories titled "Crossroads" which he hadn't started yet, so he got a beer and sat down in his favorite chair to read.

He loved the twists and turns of the stories and finished the entire book by dinner time. He got another beer, heated up a frozen pizza, and sat down to watch a little TV. He changed the dressing and added more antibiotic cream to the cut that had continued to bleed throughout the day. "It just needs more time to heal," he whispered and placed a tighter wrap around his hand before going to bed.

He fell asleep quickly, but he didn't sleep well. He dreamed about his wound and of the shadows that moved within his garage. He dreamed that the gash on his hand was much worse than he had thought and it continued to bleed out onto his sheets. He needed to get to the doctor for stitches and when he went out to get in his car, he discovered he had left the car on with the window open and the air conditioner running.

"Shit! That damn snake will have crawled into the window to get to the cold air," he cried. But he had to get to the doctor, so he ran toward the car. Not seeing anything in the front or back seat he quickly got in and flipped the switch that closed the window. He pulled out of the garage and thought how lucky he was. He was several miles from the Urgent Care center when he felt something on his foot. He was frozen as he could feel the snake crawling up his leg and when its head appeared just above his knee, he screamed.

The scream woke him and as he saw the sun shining through the window, he realized it was only a dream. But then he saw the blood that had oozed out onto the sheets throughout the night. He yelled "Shit!" again as he examined his bloody hand and understood he really was going to have to go to the Urgent Care center to get stitches. He cleaned his hand, applied another bandage, and got dressed, all the while thinking, if his car was actually running when he got to the door of the garage, he would just have to call an Uber.

The car was not on though, so he sighed with relief and cautiously inched his way toward it. He kept his eyes on the corner of the garage where he had seen movement and noticed that a small paint can had been turned over and what looked like a dirty garden hose was slithering around the garden equipment. He jumped into his car and locked the door.

He opened the garage door and left it open, thinking the snake would probably leave on its own and so he drove away, believing that his idea was a good one. His hand needed five stitches and the doctor told him to try and keep from moving it a lot over the next forty-eight hours. All the way home he thought about the snake and hoped it was gone. He parked his car just outside of the garage and got out and stared into the corner of the garage before going any further.

He knew he couldn't stay out there forever, so he grabbed a pickax off the wall and walked toward the corner.

"Come on out!" he screamed as he moved closer to the empty garden pots and shoved them once with the pickax. Nothing moved but the garden pots and his intestine which flipped over several times, but there was no black serpentine shadow. He moved the pots away with the ax and saw that there was nothing there and he smiled as he thought of how well his idea had worked. He then drove his car into the garage and went into the house. Once inside, he drank a beer with a victorious swagger.

A week later, his hand was doing much better and he needed to go to the grocery store. As a precaution, he looked to the corner of the garage and when he saw nothing, he laughed at his paranoia and drove away. Upon his return, he glanced over at the ceramic pots once again, more out of habit than concern. But this time he saw a small paint can had once again been pushed over and he knew the snake had returned. He ran into the house and knew he would have to deal with this problem once and for all.

Henry sat down and researched the subject of venomous snakes within the Central Savannah Area and found that there were six: the Timber rattlesnake, the Eastern Diamondback rattlesnake, the Pigmy rattlesnake, the Copperhead, the Eastern Coral snake, and the Water Moccasin. Based upon what he read, and what he had seen and heard in his garage, he was pretty sure that there wasn't a rattlesnake out there, but he wasn't sure about the other three. And he knew he didn't want to get close enough to find out.

As he wondered what he would do, he finally devised a plan that he thought was quite ingenious for a person who was deathly afraid of snakes. He would grab his pole saw from the garage and start it outside. Once it was running, he would move toward the corner of the garage and whatever got chopped up in the process of eliminating this threat, well, he would just have to accept that. He put on his leather gloves and his safety glasses and started the saw. As he moved closer toward the corner of the garage, he saw something dark and rope-like move and he pushed the saw toward it. He felt like he was cutting through a tough sinewy cord and he moved the saw up and down and sideways until he was certain whatever he was cutting into, had been 'killed' multiple times.

When he moved the pots back, he could see a small part of the snake still wrapped around the saw. He re-engaged the steel chain until what was left was mainly a collection of unrecognizable molecules, except for some snake-like segments that were stuck to the wall and the blood splatters that were all over the wall and floor, as well as his tools, pants, and shoes. He didn't care. It was a snake and it was trespassing and had taken his anxiety level into a manic stage, and he was glad he had killed it.

After he cleaned up the mess, he decided he would celebrate by doing some gardening in the yard, drinking some beers, and grilling a steak later that evening. He loaded his bloody clothes into the washer, put on a long-sleeved t-shirt, a new pair of work jeans, and work boots, and headed out to the garage. He knew it would be hot outside, especially with the long-sleeved shirt, but the shirt helped keep ticks away, so he didn't care.

While getting his garden tools, he dropped his trowel behind one of the large pots. He would have been concerned about doing that just thirty minutes ago, but he knew he had eliminated the menace so he reached down for the trowel. It immediately felt as if someone had driven two nails into his hand. He jerked his hand back and his shirt got caught on a small bundle of barbed wire that he kept in that area. As he tried to remove his shirt from the barbed entanglement, he felt the nails enter his hand again.

He saw the dark menacing shape and he swiped at it with his right hand only to feel the angry spikes enter his forearm as if someone had shot him with a nail gun. The pain was so intense that he ripped his left hand free of the barbed wire. That's when he saw the full image of the grayish-black snake, staring at him, coiled to strike again, if he made any more threatening movements. It had already been stressed numerous times and was in a foul mood.

Henry had failed to realize that the Eastern Black King snake he had killed with the pole saw was not seeking shelter; it was hunting for food. It had followed the Water Moccasin into the garage several times to try and get it. The venom from this very large snake, went directly into Henry's veins three times; twice into the venous network of vessels on his left hand and the third time, into the basilic vein in his right arm when he reacted so foolishly. The extremely high volume of poison was moving quickly and was already creating life-threatening reactions within his body. He was able to stumble into the house, retrieve his car keys and even open the garage door and start the car, but that was as far as he got.

His neighbors found him about a week later after they smelled something rotten and noticed Henry's garage door had been left open for several days. Once the car had run out of gas, it essentially became a large oven due to the heat and helped cook Henry's body that was suffering from severe tissue necrosis and coagulation issues from the multiple snake bites, which ultimately caused the skin on his hands and arms to swell and burst apart.

The splatter of Henry's body inside the car was much worse than what he had accomplished with the pole saw and the Black King snake. If he would have only left it alone, his worries, born of ignorance and fear, about a poisonous snake would have been resolved. But sometimes we let our fears control our actions and when that occurs, nothing good usually happens.

The Two Brothers

There were once upon a time two brothers, one rich and the other poor. The rich one was a goldsmith and evil-hearted. The poor one supported himself by making brooms and was good and honorable. The poor one had two children, who were twin brothers and as like each other as two drops of water. The two boys went backwards and forwards to the rich house and often got some of the scraps to eat. It happened once when the poor man was going into the forest to fetch brush-wood, that he saw a bird which was quite golden and more beautiful than any he had ever chanced to meet with. He picked up a small stone, threw it at him, and was lucky enough to hit him, but one golden feather only fell down, and the bird flew away. The man took the feather and carried it to his brother, who looked at it and said, "It is pure gold!" and gave him a great deal of money for it. The next day the man climbed into a birch tree and was about to cut off a couple of branches when the same bird flew out. When the man searched he found a nest, and an egg lay inside it, which was of gold. He took the egg home with him and carried it to his brother, who again said, "It is pure gold," and gave him what it was worth. At last, the goldsmith said, "I should indeed like to have the bird itself." The poor man went into the forest for the third time, and again saw the golden bird sitting on the tree, so he took a stone and brought it down and carried it to his brother, who gave him a great heap of gold for it. "Now I can get on," thought he, and went contentedly home.

The goldsmith was crafty and cunning and knew very well what kind of a bird it was. He called his wife and said, "Roast me the gold bird, and take care that none of it is lost. I have a fancy to eat it all myself." The bird, however, was no common one, but of so wondrous a kind that whosoever ate its heart and liver found every morning a piece of gold beneath his pillow. The woman made the bird ready, put it on the spit, and let it roast. Now it happened that while it was at the fire, and the woman was forced to go out of the kitchen on account of some other work, the two children of the poor broom-maker ran in, stood by the spit, and turned it round once or twice. And as at that very moment, two little bits of the bird fell down into the dripping-tin, one of the boys said, "We will eat these two little bits; I am so hungry, and no one will ever miss them." Then the two ate the pieces, but the woman came into the kitchen and saw that they were eating something and said, "What have ye been eating?"

"Two little morsels which fell out of the bird," answered they, "That must have been the heart and the liver," said the woman, quite frightened, and in order that her husband might not miss them and be angry, she quickly killed a young cock, took out his heart and liver, and put them beside the golden bird. When it was ready, she carried it to the goldsmith, who consumed it all alone and left none of it. Next morning, however, when he felt beneath his pillow and expected to bring out the piece of gold, no more gold pieces were there than there had always been.

The two children did not know what a piece of good fortune had fallen to their lot. The next morning when they arose, something fell rattling to the ground, and when they picked it up, there were two gold pieces! They took them to their father, who was astonished and said, "How can that have happened?" When next morning they again found two, and so on daily, he went to his brother and told him the strange story. The goldsmith at once knew how it had come to pass, and that the children had eaten the heart and liver of the golden bird. In order to revenge himself, and because he was envious and hard-hearted, he said to the father, "Thy children are in league with the Evil One, do not take the gold, and do not suffer them to stay any longer in thy house, for he has them in his power, and may ruin thee likewise." The father feared the Evil One, and painful as it was to him, he nevertheless led the twins forth into the forest, and with a sad heart left them there.

And now the two children ran about the forest, and sought the way home again, but could not find it, and only lost themselves more and more. At length, they met with a huntsman, who asked, "To whom do you children belong?" "We are the poor broom-maker's boys," they replied, and they told him that their father would not keep them any longer in the house because a piece of gold lay every morning under their pillows. "Come," said the huntsman, "that is nothing so very bad, if at the same time you keep honest, and are not idle." As the good man liked the children and had none of his own, he took them home with him and said, "I will be your father, and bring you up till you are big." They learned huntsmanship from him, and the piece of gold which each of them found when he awoke, was kept for them by him in case they should need it in the future.

When they were grown up, their foster-father one day took them into the forest with him, and said, "Today shall you make your trial shot, so that I may release you from your apprenticeship, and make you huntsmen." They went with him to lie in wait and stayed there a long time, but no game appeared. The huntsman, however, looked above him and saw a covey of wild geese flying in the form of a triangle, and said to one of them, "Shoot me down one from each corner." He did it and thus accomplished his trial shot. Soon after another covey came flying by in the form of the figure two, and the huntsman bade the other also bring down one from each corner, and his trial shot was likewise successful. "Now," said the foster-father, "I pronounce you out of your apprenticeship; you are skilled huntsmen."

Thereupon the two brothers went forth together into the forest, and took counsel with each other and planned something. And in the evening when they had sat down to supper, they said to their foster-father, "We will not touch food, or take one mouthful until you have granted us a request." Said he, "What, then, is your request?" They replied, "We have now finished learning, and we must prove ourselves in the world, so allow us to go away and travel." Then spake the old man joyfully, "You talk like brave huntsmen, that which you desire has been my wish; go forth, all will go well with you." Thereupon they ate and drank joyously together.

When the appointed day came, their foster-father presented each of them with a good gun and a dog, and let each of them take as many of his saved-up gold pieces as he chose. Then he accompanied them a part of the way, and when taking leave, he gave them a bright knife, and said, "If ever you separate, stick this knife into a tree at the place where you part, and when one of you goes back, he will be able to see how his absent brother is faring. For the side of the knife which is turned in the direction by which he went, will rust if he dies, but will remain bright as long as he is alive." The two brothers went still farther onwards and came to a forest which was so large that it was impossible for them to get out of it in one day. So they passed the night in it and ate what they had put in their hunting-pouches, but they walked all the second day likewise, and still did not get out. As they had nothing left to eat, one of them said, "We must shoot something for ourselves or we shall suffer from hunger," and loaded his gun, and looked about him. And when an old hare came running up towards them, he laid his gun on his shoulder, but the hare cried,

> "Dear huntsman, do but let me live,
> Two little ones to thee I'll give,"

and sprang instantly into the thicket, and brought two young ones. But the little creatures played so merrily, and were so pretty, that the huntsmen could not find it in their hearts to kill them. They, therefore, kept them with them, and the little hares followed on foot. Soon after this, a fox crept past; they were just going to shoot it, but the fox cried,

> "Dear huntsman, do but let me live,
> Two little ones I'll also give."

He, too, brought two little foxes, and the huntsmen did not like to kill them either but gave them to the hares for company, and they followed behind. It was not long before a wolf strode out of the thicket; the huntsmen made ready to shoot him, but the wolf cried,

> "Dear huntsman, do but let me live,
> Two little ones I'll likewise give."

The huntsmen put the two wolves beside the other animals, and they followed behind them. Then a bear came who wanted to trot about a little longer, and cried:

> "Dear huntsman, do but let me live,
> Two little ones I, too, will give."

The two young bears were added to the others, and there were already eight of them. At length who came? A lion came and tossed his mane. But the huntsmen did not let themselves be frightened and aimed at him likewise, but the lion also said,

> "Dear huntsman, do but let me live,
> Two little ones I, too, will give."

And he brought his little ones to them, and now the huntsmen had two lions, two bears, two wolves, two foxes, and two hares, who followed them and served them. In the meantime, their hunger was not appeased by this, and they said to the foxes, "Hark ye, cunning fellows, provide us with something to eat. You are crafty and deep." They replied, "Not far from here lies a village, from which we have already brought many a fowl; we will show you the way there." So, they went into the village, bought themselves something to eat, had some food given to their beasts, and then traveled onwards. The foxes, however, knew their way very well about the district and where the poultry yards were and were able to guide the huntsmen.

Now they traveled about for a while, but could find no situations where they could remain together, so they said, "There is nothing else for it, we must part." They divided the animals so that each of them had a lion, a bear, a wolf, a fox, and a hare. Then they took leave of each other, promised to love each other like brothers till their death, and stuck the knife which their foster-father had given them, into a tree, after which one went east, and the other went west.

The younger, however, arrived with his beasts in a town that was all hung with black crepe. He went into an inn and asked the host if he could accommodate his animals. The innkeeper gave him a stable, where there was a hole in the wall, and the hare crept out and fetched himself the head of a cabbage, and the fox fetched himself a hen, and when he had devoured that got the cock as well, but the wolf, the bear, and the lion could not get out because they were too big. Then the innkeeper let them be taken to a place where a cow was just then lying on the grass, that they might eat till they were satisfied. And when the huntsman had taken care of his animals, he asked the innkeeper why the town was thus hung with black crepe? Said the host, "Because our King's only daughter is to die tomorrow." The huntsman inquired if she was "sick unto death?" "No," answered the host, "she is vigorous and healthy, nevertheless she must die!"

"How is that?" asked the huntsman. "There is a high hill without the town, whereon dwells a dragon who every year must have a pure virgin, or he lays the whole country waste, and now all the maidens have already been given to him, and there is no longer anyone left but the King's daughter. Yet there is no mercy for her; she must be given up to him, and that is to be done tomorrow." Said the huntsman, "Why is the dragon not killed?" "Ah," replied the host, "so many knights have tried it, but it has cost all of them their lives. The King has promised that he who conquers the dragon shall have his daughter to wife, and shall likewise govern the kingdom after his own death."

The huntsman said nothing more to this, but next morning took his animals, and with them ascended the dragon's hill. A little church stood at the top of it, and on the altar, three full cups were standing, with the inscription, "Whosoever empties the cups will become the strongest man on earth and will be able to wield the sword which is buried before the threshold of the door." The huntsman did not drink, but went out and sought for the sword in the ground, but was unable to move it from its place. Then he went in and emptied the cups, and now he was strong enough to take up the sword, and his hand could quite easily wield it. When the hour came when the maiden was to be delivered over to the dragon, the King, the marshal, and courtiers accompanied her. From afar she saw the huntsman on the dragon's hill, and thought it was the dragon standing there waiting for her, and did not want to go up to him, but at last, because otherwise the whole town would have been destroyed, she was forced to go the miserable journey. The King and courtiers returned home full of grief; the King's marshal, however, was to stand still and see all from a distance.

When the King's daughter got to the top of the hill, it was not the dragon which stood there, but the young huntsman, who comforted her, and said he would save her. He led her into the church and locked her in. It was not long before the seven-headed dragon came thither with loud roaring. When he perceived the huntsman, he was astonished and said, "What business hast thou here on the hill?" The huntsman answered, "I want to fight with thee." Said the dragon, "Many knights have left their lives here, I shall soon have made an end of thee too," and he breathed fire out of seven jaws.

The fire was to have lighted the dry grass, and the huntsman was to have been suffocated in the heat and smoke, but the animals came running up and trampled out the fire. Then the dragon rushed upon the huntsman, but he swung his sword until it sang through the air, and struck off three of his heads. Then the dragon grew right furious, and rose up in the air, and spat out flames of fire over the huntsman, and was about to plunge down on him, but the huntsman once more drew out his sword and again cut off three of his heads. The monster became faint and sank down, nevertheless, it was just able to rush upon the huntsman. But he with his last strength smote its tail off, and as he could fight no longer, called up his animals who tore it in pieces.

When the struggle was ended, the huntsman unlocked the church and found the King's daughter lying on the floor, as she had lost her senses with anguish and terror during the contest. He carried her out, and when she came to herself once more and opened her eyes, he showed her the dragon all cut to pieces and told her that she was now delivered. She rejoiced and said, "Now thou wilt be my dearest husband, for my father has promised me to him who kills the dragon." Thereupon she took off her necklace of coral and divided it amongst the animals in order to reward them, and the lion received the golden clasp. Her pocket handkerchief, however, on which was her name, she gave to the huntsman, who went and cut the tongues out of the dragon's seven heads, wrapped them in the handkerchief, and preserved them carefully.

That done, as he was so faint and weary with the fire and the battle, he said to the maiden, "We are both faint and weary, we will

72

sleep awhile." Then she said, "yes," and they lay down on the ground, and the huntsman said to the lion, "Thou shalt keep watch, that no one surprises us in our sleep," and both fell asleep. The lion lay down beside them to watch, but he also was so weary with the fight, that he called to the bear and said, "Lie down near me, I must sleep a little: if anything comes, waken me." Then the bear lay down beside him, but he also was tired, and called the wolf and said, "Lie down by me, I must sleep a little, but if anything comes, waken me." Then the wolf lay down by him, but he was tired likewise, and called the fox and said, "Lie down by me, I must sleep a little; if anything comes, waken me." Then the fox lay down beside him, but he too was weary, and called the hare and said, "Lie down near me, I must sleep a little, and if anything should come, waken me." Then the hare sat down by him, but the poor hare was tired too, and had no one whom he could call there to keep watch, and fell asleep. And now the King's daughter, the huntsman, the lion, the bear, the wolf, the fox, and the hare, were all sleeping a sound sleep. The marshal, however, who was to look on from a distance, took courage when he did not see the dragon flying away with the maiden, and finding that all the hill had become quiet, ascended it.

There lay the dragon hacked and hewn to pieces on the ground, and not far from it were the King's daughter and a huntsman with his animals, and all of them were sunk in a sound sleep. And as he was wicked and godless, he took his sword, cut off the huntsman's head, and seized the maiden in his arms, and carried her down the hill. Then she awoke and was terrified, but the marshal said, "Thou art in my hands, thou shalt say that it was I who killed the dragon." "I cannot do that," she replied, "for it was a huntsman with his animals who did it." Then he drew his sword, and threatened to kill her if she did not obey him, and so compelled her that she promised it. Then he took her to the King, who did not know how to contain himself for joy when he once more looked on his dear child in life, whom he had believed to have been torn to pieces by the monster. The marshal said to him, "I have killed the dragon and delivered the maiden and the whole kingdom as well, therefore I demand her

73

as my wife, as was promised." The King said to the maiden, "Is what he says true?" "Ah, yes," she answered, "it must indeed be true, but I will not consent to have the wedding celebrated until after a year and a day," for she thought in that time she should hear something of her dear huntsman.

The animals, however, were still lying sleeping beside their dead master on the dragon's hill, and there came a great humble-bee and lighted on the hare's nose, but the hare wiped it off with his paw and went on sleeping. The humble-bee came a second time, but the hare again rubbed it off and slept on. Then it came for the third time and stung his nose so that he awoke. As soon as the hare was awake, he roused the fox, and the fox, the wolf, and the wolf, the bear, and the bear, the lion. And when the lion awoke and saw that the maiden was gone, and his master was dead, he began to roar frightfully and cried, "Who has done that? Bear, why didst thou not waken me?" The bear asked the wolf, "Why didst thou not waken me?" and the wolf the fox, "Why didst thou not waken me?" and the fox the hare, "Why didst thou not waken me?" The poor hare alone did not know what answer to make, and the blame rested with him. Then they were just going to fall upon him, but he entreated them and said, "Kill me not, I will bring our master to life again. I know a mountain on which a root grows which, when placed in the mouth of anyone, cures him of all illness and every wound. But the mountain lies two hundred hours journey from here."

The lion said, "In four-and-twenty hours must thou have run thither and have come back, and have brought the root with thee." Then the hare sprang away, and in four-and-twenty hours he was back and brought the root with him. The lion put the huntsman's head on again, and the hare placed the root in his mouth, and immediately everything united together again, and his heart beat, and life came back. Then the huntsman awoke, and was alarmed when he did not see the maiden, and thought, "She must have gone away whilst I was sleeping, in order to get rid of me." The lion in

74

his great haste had put his master's head on the wrong way round, but the huntsman did not observe it because of his melancholy thoughts about the King's daughter. But at noon, when he was going to eat something, he saw that his head was turned backwards and could not understand it, and asked the animals what had happened to him in his sleep. Then the lion told him that they, too, had all fallen asleep from weariness, and on awaking, had found him dead with his head cut off, that the hare had brought the life-giving root, and that he, in his haste, had laid hold of the head the wrong way, but that he would repair his mistake. Then he tore the huntsman's head off again, turned it round, and the hare healed it with the root.

The huntsman, however, was sad at heart, and traveled about the world, and made his animals dance before people. It came to pass that precisely at the end of one year he came back to the same town where he had delivered the King's daughter from the dragon, and this time the town was gaily hung with red cloth. Then he said to the host, "What does this mean? Last year the town was all hung with black crepe, what means the red cloth today?" The host answered, "Last year our King's daughter was to have been delivered over to the dragon, but the marshal fought with it and killed it, and so tomorrow their wedding is to be solemnized, and that is why the town was then hung with black crepe for mourning and is today covered with red cloth for joy!"

Next day when the wedding was to take place, the huntsman said at mid-day to the innkeeper, "Do you believe, sir host, that I while with you here today shall eat bread from the King's own table?" "Nay," said the host, "I would bet a hundred pieces of gold that that will not come true." The huntsman accepted the wager and set against it a purse with just the same number of gold pieces. Then he called the hare and said, "Go, my dear runner, and fetch me some of the bread which the King is eating." Now the little hare was the lowest of the animals, and could not transfer this order to any of the others, but had to get on his legs himself. "Alas!" thought he, "if I bound through the streets thus alone, the butchers' dogs will all be after me." It happened as he expected, and the dogs came after him and wanted to make holes in his good skin. But he sprang away (have you have never seen one running?) and sheltered himself in a sentry-box without the soldier being aware of it. Then the dogs came and wanted to have him out, but the soldier did not understand a jest and struck them with the butt-end of his gun till they ran away yelling and howling. As soon as the hare saw that the way was clear, he ran into the palace and straight to the King's daughter, sat down under her chair, and scratched at her foot. Then she said, "Wilt thou get away?" and thought it was her dog. The hare scratched her foot for the second time, and she again said, "Wilt thou get away?" and thought it was her dog. But the hare did not let itself be turned from its purpose and scratched her for the third time. Then she peeped down and knew the hare by its collar.

She took him on her lap, carried him into her chamber, and said, "Dear Hare, what dost thou want?" He answered, "My master, who killed the dragon, is here, and has sent me to ask for a loaf of bread like that which the King eats." Then she was full of joy and had the baker summoned, and ordered him to bring a loaf such as was eaten by the King. The little hare said, "But the baker must likewise carry it thither for me, that the butchers' dogs may do no harm to me." The baker carried it for him as far as the door of the inn, and then the hare got on his hind legs, took the loaf in his front paws, and carried it to his master. Then said the huntsman, "Behold, sir host, the hundred pieces of gold are mine." The host was astonished, but the huntsman went on to say, "Yes, sir host, I have the bread, but now I will likewise have some of the King's roast meat."

The host said, "I should indeed like to see that," but he would make no more wagers. The huntsman called the fox and said, "My little fox, go and fetch me some roast meat, such as the King eats."

76

The red fox knew the by-ways better and went by holes and corners without any dog seeing him, seated himself under the chair of the King's daughter, and scratched her foot. Then she looked down and recognized the fox by its collar, took him into her chamber with her and said, "Dear fox, what dost thou want?" He answered, "My master, who killed the dragon, is here, and has sent me. I am to ask for some roast meat such as the King is eating." Then she made the cook come, who was obliged to prepare a roast joint, the same as was eaten by the King, and to carry it for the fox as far as the door. Then the fox took the dish, waved away with his tail the flies which had settled on the meat, and then carried it to his master. "Behold, sir host," said the huntsman, "bread and meat are here but now I will also have proper vegetables with it, such as are eaten by the King." Then he called the wolf, and said, "Dear Wolf, go thither and fetch me vegetables such as the King eats."

Then the wolf went straight to the palace, as he feared no one, and when he got to the King's daughter's chamber, he twitched at the back of her dress, so that she was forced to look round. She recognized him by his collar, and took him into her chamber with her, and said, "Dear Wolf, what dost thou want?" He answered, "My master, who killed the dragon, is here, I am to ask for some vegetables, such as the King eats." Then she made the cook come, and he had to make ready a dish of vegetables, such as the King ate and had to carry it for the wolf as far as the door, and then the wolf took the dish from him and carried it to his master. "Behold, sir host," said the huntsman, "now I have bread and meat and vegetables, but I will also have some pastry to eat like that which the King eats." He called the bear, and said, "Dear Bear, thou art fond of licking anything sweet; go and bring me some confectionery, such as the King eats."

Then the bear trotted to the palace, and everyone got out of his way, but when he went to the guard, they presented their muskets, and would not let him go into the royal palace. But he got up on his hind legs, and gave them a few boxes on the ears, right and left, with his paws, so that the whole watch broke up, and then he went straight to the King's daughter, placed himself behind her, and growled a little. Then she looked behind her, knew the bear, and bade him go into her room with her, and said, "Dear Bear, what dost thou want?" He answered, "My master, who killed the dragon, is here, and I am to ask for some confectionery, such as the King eats." Then she summoned her confectioner, who had to bake confectionery such as the King ate, and carry it to the door for the bear; then the bear first licked up the comfits which had rolled down, and then he stood upright, took the dish, and carried it to his master. "Behold, sir host," said the huntsman, "now I have bread, meat, vegetables, and confectionery, but I will drink wine also, such as the King drinks." He called his lion to him and said, "Dear Lion, thou thyself likest to drink till thou art intoxicated, go and fetch me some wine, such as is drunk by the King."

Then the lion strode through the streets, and the people fled from him, and when he came to the watch, they wanted to bar the way against him, but he did but roar once, and they all ran away. Then the lion went to the royal apartment and knocked at the door with his tail. Then the King's daughter came forth and was almost afraid of the lion, but she knew him by the golden clasp of her necklace, and bade him go with her into her chamber, and said, "Dear Lion, what wilt thou have?" He answered, "My master, who killed the dragon, is here, and I am to ask for some wine such as is drunk by the King." Then she bade the cup-bearer be called, who was to give the lion some wine like that which was drunk by the King. The lion said, "I will go with him, and see that I get the right wine." Then he went down with the cup-bearer, and when they were below, the cup-bearer wanted to draw him some of the common wine that was drunk by the King's servants, but the lion said, "Stop, I will taste the wine first," and he drew half a measure, and swallowed it down at one draught. "No," said he, "that is not right." The cup-bearer looked at him askance, but went on, and was about to give him some out of another barrel which was for the King's marshal. The lion said, "Stop, let me taste the wine first," and drew half a measure and drank it. "That is better, but still not right," said he. Then the cup-bearer grew angry and said, "How can a stupid animal like you understand wine?" But the lion gave him a blow behind the ears, which made him fall down by no means gently, and when he had got up again, he conducted the lion quite silently into a little cellar apart, where the King's wine lay, from which no one else ever drank. The lion first drew half a measure and tried the wine, and then he said, "That may possibly be the right sort," and bade the cup-bearer fill six bottles of it. And now they went upstairs again, but when the lion came out of the cellar into the open air, he reeled here and there and was rather drunk, and the cup-bearer was forced to carry the wine as far as the door for him. Then the lion took the handle of the basket in his mouth and took it to his master. The huntsman said, "Behold, sir host, here have I bread, meat, vegetables, confectionery and wine such as the King has, and now I will dine with my animals," and he sat down and ate and drank, and gave the hare, the fox, the wolf, the bear, and the lion also to eat and to drink, and was joyful, for he saw that the King's daughter still loved him. And when he had finished his dinner, he said, "Sir host, now have I eaten and drunk, as the King eats and drinks, and now I will go to the King's court and marry the King's daughter."

Said the host, "How can that be, when she already has a betrothed husband, and when the wedding is to be solemnized today?" Then the huntsman drew forth the handkerchief which the King's daughter had given him on the dragon's hill, and in which were folded the monster's seven tongues, and said, "That which I hold in my hand shall help me to do it." Then the innkeeper looked at the handkerchief, and said, "Whatever I believe, I do not believe that, and I am willing to stake my house and courtyard on it." The huntsman, however, took a bag with a thousand gold pieces, put it on the table, and said, "I stake that on it."

Now the King said to his daughter, at the royal table, "What did all the wild animals want, which have been coming to thee, and

79

going in and out of my palace?" She replied, "I may not tell you, but send and have the master of these animals brought, and you will do well." The King sent a servant to the inn and invited the stranger, and the servant came just as the huntsman had laid his wager with the innkeeper. Then said he, "Behold, sir host, now the King sends his servant and invites me, but I do not go in this way."

And he said to the servant, "I request the Lord King to send me royal clothing, and a carriage with six horses, and servants to attend me." When the King heard the answer, he said to his daughter, "What shall I do?" She said, "Cause him to be fetched as he desires to be, and you will do well." Then the King sent royal apparel, a carriage with six horses, and servants to wait on him. When the huntsman saw them coming, he said, "Behold, sir host, now I am fetched as I desired to be," and he put on the royal garments, took the handkerchief with the dragon's tongues with him, and drove off to the King.

When the King saw him coming, he said to his daughter, "How shall I receive him?" She answered, "Go to meet him and you will do well." Then the King went to meet him and led him in, and his animals followed. The King gave him a seat near himself and his daughter, and the marshal, as bridegroom, sat on the other side, but no longer knew the huntsman. And now at this very moment, the seven heads of the dragon were brought in as a spectacle, and the King said, "The seven heads were cut off the dragon by the marshal, wherefore today I give him my daughter to wife." Then the huntsman stood up, opened the seven mouths, and said, "Where are the seven tongues of the dragon?" Then was the marshal terrified, and grew pale and knew not what answer he should make. At length in his anguish, he said, "Dragons have no tongues." The huntsman said, "Liars ought to have none, but the dragon's tongues are the tokens of the victor," and he unfolded the handkerchief, and there lay all seven inside it. And he put each tongue in the mouth to which it belonged, and it fitted exactly.

Then he took the handkerchief on which the name of the princess was embroidered, and showed it to the maiden, and asked to whom she had given it, and she replied, "To him who killed the dragon." And then he called his animals, and took the collar off each of them and the golden clasp from the lion, and showed them to the maiden and asked to whom they belonged. She answered, "The necklace and golden clasp were mine, but I divided them among the animals who helped to conquer the dragon." Then spake the huntsman, "When I, tired with the fight, was resting and sleeping, the marshal came and cut off my head. Then he carried away the King's daughter and gave out that it was he who had killed the dragon. But that he lied I prove with the tongues, the handkerchief, and the necklace."

And then he related how his animals had healed him by means of a wonderful root, and how he had traveled about with them for one year and had at length again come there and had learned the treachery of the marshal by the innkeeper's story. Then the King asked his daughter, "Is it true that this man killed the dragon?"

And she answered, "Yes, it is true. Now can I reveal the wicked deed of the marshal, as it has come to light without my connivance, for he wrung from me a promise to be silent. For this reason, however, did I make the condition that the marriage should not be solemnized for a year and a day." Then the King bade twelve councillors be summoned who were to pronounce judgment on the marshal, and they sentenced him to be torn to pieces by four bulls.

The marshal was therefore executed, but the King gave his daughter to the huntsman and named him his viceroy over the whole kingdom. The wedding was celebrated with great joy, and the young King caused his father and his foster-father to be brought and loaded them with treasures. Neither did he forget the innkeeper, but sent for him and said, "Behold, sir host, I have married the King's daughter, and your house and yard are mine." The host said, "Yes, according to justice it is so." But the young King said, "It shall be done according to mercy," and told him that he should keep his house and yard and gave him the thousand pieces of gold as well.

And now the young King and Queen were thoroughly happy and lived in gladness together. He often went out hunting because it was a delight to him, and the faithful animals had to accompany him. In the neighborhood, however, there was a forest of which it was reported that it was haunted, and that whosoever did but enter it did not easily get out again. The young King, however, had a great inclination to hunt in it and let the old King have no peace until he allowed him to do so. So he rode forth with a great following, and when he came to the forest, he saw a snow-white hart and said to his people, "Wait here until I return, I want to chase that beautiful creature," and he rode into the forest after it, followed only by his animals. The attendants halted and waited until evening, but he did not return, so they rode home and told the young Queen that the young King had followed a white hart into the enchanted forest, and had not come back again. Then she was in the greatest concern about him. He, however, had still continued to ride on and on after the beautiful wild animal, and had never been able to overtake it; when he thought he was near enough to aim, he instantly saw it bound away into the far distance, and at length, it vanished altogether.

And now he perceived that he had penetrated deep into the forest, and blew his horn but he received no answer, for his attendants could not hear it. And as night, too, was falling, he saw that he could not get home that day, so he dismounted from his horse, lighted himself a fire near a tree, and resolved to spend the night by it. While he was sitting by the fire, and his animals also were lying down beside him, it seemed to him that he heard a human voice. He looked round but could perceive nothing. Soon afterward, he again heard a groan as if from above, and then he looked up and saw an old woman sitting in the tree, who wailed unceasingly, "Oh, oh, oh, how cold I am!" Said he, "Come down,

82

and warm thyself if thou art cold." But she said, "No, thy animals will bite me." He answered, "They will do thee no harm, old mother, do come down." She, however, was a witch, and said, "I will throw down a wand from the tree, and if thou strikest them on the back with it, they will do me no harm." Then she threw him a small wand, and he struck them with it, and instantly they lay still and were turned into stone. And when the witch was safe from the animals, she leapt down and touched him also with a wand, and changed him to stone. Thereupon she laughed and dragged him and the animals into a vault, where many more such stones already lay.

As, however, the young King did not come back at all, the Queen's anguish and care grew constantly greater. And it so happened that at this very time the other brother who had turned to the east when they separated, came into the kingdom. He had sought a situation, and had found none, and had then traveled about here and there, and had made his animals dance. Then it came into his mind that he would just go and look at the knife that they had thrust in the trunk of a tree at their parting, that he might learn how his brother was. When he got there his brother's side of the knife was half rusted and half bright. Then he was alarmed and thought, "A great misfortune must have befallen my brother, but perhaps I can still save him, for half the knife is still bright." He and his animals traveled towards the west, and when he entered the gate of the town, the guard came to meet him, and asked if he was to announce him to his consort the young Queen, who had for a couple of days been in the greatest sorrow about his staying away, and was afraid he had been killed in the enchanted forest?

The sentries, indeed, thought no otherwise than that he was the young King himself, for he looked so like him, and had wild animals running behind him. Then he saw that they were speaking of his brother, and thought, "It will be better if I pass myself off for him, and then I can rescue him more easily." So he allowed himself to be escorted into the castle by the guard and was received with the greatest joy. The young Queen indeed thought that he was her husband, and asked him why he had stayed away so long. He answered, "I had lost myself in a forest, and could not find my way out again any sooner." At night he was taken to the royal bed, but he laid a two-edged sword between him and the young Queen; she did not know what that could mean, but did not venture to ask.

He remained in the palace a couple of days, and in the meantime inquired into everything which related to the enchanted forest, and at last he said, "I must hunt there once more." The King and the young Queen wanted to persuade him not to do it, but he stood out against them and went forth with a larger following. When he had got into the forest, it fared with him as with his brother; he saw a white hart and said to his people, "Stay here, and wait until I return, I want to chase the lovely wild beast," and then he rode into the forest and his animals ran after him. But he could not overtake the hart, and got so deep into the forest that he was forced to pass the night there. And when he had lighted a fire, he heard someone wailing above him, "Oh, oh, oh, how cold I am!"

Then he looked up, and the self-same witch was sitting in the tree. Said he, "If thou art cold, come down, little old mother, and warm thyself." She answered, "No, thy animals will bite me." But he said, "They will not hurt thee." Then she cried, "I will throw down a wand to thee, and if thou smitest them with it they will do me no harm." When the huntsman heard that, he had no confidence in the old woman, and said, "I will not strike my animals. Come down, or I will fetch thee." Then she cried, "What dost thou want? Thou shalt not touch me." But he replied, "If thou dost not come, I will shoot thee." Said she, "Shoot away, I do not fear thy bullets!"

Then he aimed and fired at her, but the witch was proof against all leaden bullets, and laughed and yelled and cried, "Thou shalt not hit me." The huntsman knew what to do, tore three silver buttons off his coat, and loaded his gun with them, for against them her arts were useless, and when he fired she fell down at once with a scream. Then he set his foot on her and said, "Old witch, if thou dost not instantly confess where my brother is, I will seize thee with both my hands and throw thee into the fire." She was in a great fright, begged for mercy, and said, "He and his animals lie in a vault, turned to stone." Then he compelled her to go thither with him, threatened her, and said, "Old sea-cat, now shalt thou make my brother and all the human beings lying here, alive again, or thou shalt go into the fire!" She took a wand and touched the stones, and then his brother with his animals came to life again; and many others, merchants, artisans, and shepherds, arose, thanked him for their deliverance, and went to their homes. But when the twin brothers saw each other again, they kissed each other and rejoiced with all their hearts. Then they seized the witch, bound her, and laid her on the fire. When she was burnt, the forest opened of its own accord and was light and clear, and the King's palace could be seen at about the distance of a three hours walk.

Thereupon the two brothers went home together, and on the way told each other their histories. And when the youngest said that he was ruler of the whole country in the King's stead, the other observed, "That I remarked very well, for when I came to the town and was taken for thee, all royal honours were paid me; the young Queen looked on me as her husband, and I had to eat at her side, and sleep in thy bed." When the other heard that, he became so jealous and angry that he drew his sword, and struck off his brother's head. But when he saw him lying there dead and saw his red blood flowing, he repented most violently: "My brother delivered me," cried he, "and I have killed him for it," and he bewailed him aloud. Then his hare came and offered to go and bring some of the root of life, and bounded away and brought it while yet there was time, and the dead man was brought to life again and knew nothing about the wound.

After this, they journeyed onwards, and the youngest said, "Thou lookest like me, hast royal apparel on as I have, and the animals follow thee as they do me; we will go in by opposite gates, and arrive at the same time from the two sides in the aged King's presence." So they separated, and at the same time came the watchmen from the one door and from the other, and announced that the young King and the animals had returned from the chase.

The King said, "It is not possible, the gates lie quite a mile apart." In the meantime, however, the two brothers entered the courtyard of the palace from opposite sides, and both mounted the steps. Then the King said to the daughter, "Say which is thy husband. Each of them looks exactly like the other, I cannot tell." Then she was in great distress, and could not tell; but at last, she remembered the necklace which she had given to the animals, and she sought for and found her little golden clasp on the lion, and she cried in her delight, "He who is followed by this lion is my true husband." Then the young King laughed and said, "Yes, he is the right one," and they sat down together to table, and ate and drank and were merry. At night when the young King went to bed, his wife said, "Why hast thou for these last nights always laid a two-edged sword in our bed? I thought thou hadst a wish to kill me." Then he knew how true his brother had been.

The Color of Clouds

Once upon a time, there was a young wife who realized she had made some very poor choices in her life. She married at the age of sixteen, against her mother's wishes. At first, she thought she loved the man but soon realized that she didn't. At first, she just liked the way he looked and wanted to have sex with him, but after several years, the act became more of a chore than a pleasure. At first, she enjoyed having her own house, but then she realized it constantly needed cleaning, and she hated cleaning. At first, she thought she loved having two sons, but as they began to grow up, she realized she hated having two other people who depended on her.

Thus, she became a bitter and angry person. She despised the fact that her husband worked in the coal mines and came home filthy from work every evening. She started making him wash himself with a hose before she would allow him to come inside the house, which was a very cold process in a West Virginia winter. She hated that her children were now nine and eleven years old and she was left to teach them how to read because there was no school close enough to their remote home in the mountains.

She hated that part the most because her youngest son, Edwyn, seemed incapable of learning. She thought he was stupid and she could not hide the fact that looking at him reminded her of the foolish actions she had taken. She bullied her son and her husband, often berating both of them for their stupidity and the poor living conditions in which she had to endure. Her oldest son, Tristan, saw how his mother acted and because he didn't want to suffer her indignities, he became very much like her. It wasn't long before the daily routine consisted of the mother telling her husband how she hated her life and listing all the things that he failed to provide her, and Tristan telling Edwyn how useless he was and how he wouldn't "grow up to be worth spit."

Though he didn't want to leave his youngest son in this household under these conditions, Edwyn's father elected to serve his country at this time in the world's history. It was 1943 and Edwyn's father enlisted in the Navy. He was assigned to the U.S.S. Laffey, a destroyer that was soon to be a major part of the invasion of France and later an integral component of the 7th fleet in the Pacific and the battle of Okinawa. Because of his mining background, he was assigned to the fire branch and eventually became a Fire Controller 1st class. He had seen tragic accidents within the mines, but nothing that he had witnessed in his past would prepare him for what he encountered on this ship.

While his father was away, Edwyn suffered daily. His only comfort was found in the woods and he went there as often as he could to get away from his mother and brother. It was during one of those trips to the woods that he stumbled upon a sick puppy that appeared to be almost dead. Edwyn wasn't sure what to do until he heard a kind voice behind him saying, "That pup's been abandoned by its mother and left out here to die." When Edwyn turned around, he saw an old man standing before him, leaning on a large wooden pole and looking down at him with a smile.

"If you pick it up, we can take it back to my cabin and give it some goat's milk. If he survives that, in five or six weeks, we can start feeding it some solid food. Would you want to try that, boy?"

Edwyn nodded and picked up the starved and near-dead puppy and followed the man to his small home beside a stream and large rocks. His cabin was so well hidden, Edwyn would never have found it by himself. The closer he walked toward it, the more it seemed to disappear into the forest as if dark storm clouds had moved into the tops of the trees around it and blotted out the sun and the home's existence.

He took Edwyn into his house and had him lay the pup down on a soft fur rug. Edwyn followed him out to the back of the cabin where the man had two goats and a cow. He showed Edwyn how to milk the goat and then had him carry it back inside. Edwyn wasn't sure how he would get the milk into the pup's mouth when the man handed him a copper funnel.

"First, put some milk on your finger and let it drip into the pup's mouth. If he starts to swallow it, then it ain't too late. If that doesn't arouse him, then I'm afraid, boy, the dog wasn't meant for this world."

Edwyn did what the old man told him, and he closed his eyes and prayed that the pup would start drinking the milk. His prayer was answered and as soon as the old man saw the pup was taking the milk from his finger, he put a thin cloth around the end of the funnel and told Edwyn to hold it tight while he poured a little of the goat's milk into it. The cloth allowed a steady drip into the pup's mouth and he drank every bit of it until the old man told him that was enough for now and to let the pup rest.

The old man sat down and told Edwyn he had a way with animals that most people didn't possess. He said the goat was usually an "ornery old cuss," but it didn't seem to mind him getting the milk at all, and that pup seemed to know he didn't mean it no harm and that just didn't happen with everyone. "Animals can sense things about people. They know who will harm them and who won't. The animals like you son, and you should take joy in that."

Edwyn was uncomfortable with compliments as he had only heard his father say a kind word to him every so often, and that was usually a "sorry" or a "stay strong" and so he bowed his head in embarrassment.

"No need to do that, Edwyn. You are a good boy. A strong boy," the old man said. Edwyn looked at him with surprise, not understanding how this stranger knew his name.

The old man recognized that surprised look and laughed.

"I know your name, boy, because your father and I go back a bit. I've known your father Conrad since he was a little boy. He goes by Connie now and I know he's off fighting in the war. He was always a brave young boy and young man too. Smart too, except for picking that wife of his. Claudia," he said and then spit into a can that was next to his chair. "Named after her father Claude. He wasn't much of a father, so I suppose some people would say, the acorn don't fall too far from the tree with regard to her. He was mean and so is she. By the way, my name is Caleb. My friends call me Caleb," he said as he winked at Edwyn.

"Would you like some cold water? Got a pump handle out in front of the house that draws up water from a sweet well. Some of the best water in these hills. Got many a man, and even a few women, that say I got the best water around these parts. Take that glass jar over there on the counter, and go out and get us some water. Nothing we can do for that pup now, but in a couple of hours, he will be wanting some more milk."

Edwyn did as requested and returned with the water. Without even getting a glass to drink from, Caleb told him to just drink from the jar, and what he didn't finish, to give to him. Again, Edwyn did as ordered and he thought the old man was right as he handed him the jar. It was very good-tasting water.

"You don't say much, do you?" Caleb asked as he drank most of the water and offered him the jar again. Edwyn shook his head no and watched Caleb finish it.

Edwyn didn't know how to respond. He was only used to saying "yes ma'am," or "sorry," or "stop it." He wasn't used to having conversations with anyone, even his father, who was usually too tired and just talked about his day in the mines and how everything would be okay someday soon.

"I uh...uh...no sir, I don't...but if......if you...you don't mind me asking.....how...how long have you been here, K...K..k-leb?"

"A long time. You can tell I'm an old man by this ragged gray beard and hair, so let's just say a long time. I grew up around this place and I reckon I'll die here. But that's okay with me. Got lots of good memories."

At that time, Edwyn noticed the book shelf beside the fireplace and his eyes opened wide. He had never seen that many books in his entire life. Caleb caught sight of Edwyn's interest and suggested he go over and pick one out. Edwyn walked to the large book shelf hesitantly, fearing if he touched one of the books, it would start yelling at him like his mother or his brother, telling him he was too stupid to read. He reached over and grabbed the closest book and handed it to Caleb.

"That's a great book, Edwyn. You read 'Rip Van Winkle' or 'The Legend of Sleepy Hollow' before?"

Edwyn shook his head no.

"You like to read, don't you?"

Edwyn again shook his head no.

"You don't like to read? That's no way to get through life - not reading. I bet your mother has something to do with that and I will bet your father hasn't had the time nor the inclination to fight with your mother with regard to your book learning. Seems to me, I kind of remember him not being interested in books either at your age, and it took a while for that to change. Then he got interested in other things, like that mother of yours.

"But don't misunderstand me, Edwyn. I'm not bad-mouthing your father. He's just been tormented by that wife of his for too long. He's a good man. You need to give him time and be kind with him; I suspect even more so when he comes back from the war. Takes a brave man to go off to war, Edwyn. A very brave man. So, you be proud of your father. I know he's proud of you."

"He......he....is?"

"Oh goodness, yes. He sees a lot of himself in you. Not easy to live in a world that seems to want to beat down on you every time you get up in the morning. But your father kept going and you got an inner strength just like him."

Edwyn smiled at Caleb. It made him feel good to hear that.

"Now, back to this book you picked out. It's a good one. Couldn't have picked out a better one if I had gone over to that bookshelf myself. It's by a man named Washington Irving. Good writer and I think you would really like the stories in this book. It's called 'The Sketch Book of Geoffery Crayon, Gent.' Sort of a play on words, but I can explain all that later."

"I...can't...can't...read good. The...let...letters...look.....fun...funny. Like....look...looking in...a..mirror. The I...letters...look...b...backwards sometimes."

"Tell you what. If you would like, I can help you learn how to read and make that mirror problem become less of one. Would you want to give it a try?"

Edwyn shook his head yes.

"Let's go over there on that sofa then. Get some good light from that lamp. Here, let me turn it on. Ok, good. Now, you sit there by the light and give me the book. That's right. I'm going to read the first sentence and then you are going to read the sentence back to me and I'll explain any words that you don't understand. Here, let me show you. The title of this story is 'Rip Van Winkle' by Washington Irving. Rip Van Winkle is just the man's name. Say it," Caleb said as he pointed at the words.

"Rip......Van....Win...Wink..."

"Winkle. When you see the 'le' at the end of a word, think of a bell...and remember L. Got it?"

"Winkle."

"Yes, sir. Extree good. Now the first sentence: 'Whoever has made a voyage up the Hudson must remember the Catskill Mountains.'

"Now you say it...take the words apart if you need to...we got lots of time..."

For the next several hours, Caleb helped him read the first three pages of Rip Van Winkle and explained to him what the words meant, how to say them, and Edwyn soon began to realize that the story seemed familiar in an odd way. For the very first time, he was excited about reading and wondered how this story ended. After they finished those pages, it was time to feed the pup again. Edwyn knew what to do now and asked Caleb if he could do it by himself. Caleb smiled as he watched Edwyn feed the pup. This time after he finished the milk, the pup made a little purring noise. Edwyn seemed surprised and looked up at Caleb.

"Yeah, I heard it too. I think that pup will be okay, provided you keep taking care of him like you're doing."

Edwyn looked dejected and Caleb knew immediately what that frown meant.

"I know you can't stay down here all night. So, you get on back home and come back tomorrow. I'll watch over the pup through the night. Does that sound good? You remember how to get here, don't you?"

"Yes....yes, sir. I'll see....you tomorrow...K...K..K-leb," Edwyn replied as he jumped up and ran out the door. As soon as he started running, he turned around to go back and close the door, but Caleb was there waving and told him to go on, so Edwyn hurried home before it got dark.

His mother didn't even realize he had been gone but Tristan did and asked where he had been. Their mother gave them each a plate of cold beans and bread. Before Edwyn could respond to his brother, his mother said that she didn't want to hear any complaints from either of them about dinner because she hadn't gotten any money yet from their father. She said she wasn't sure when that damn military would get them a check but they would have to do with what they had, so she didn't want to hear any negative comments.

"I like beans and bread, momma," Tristan said.

His mother smiled as she smoked her cigarette and then looked over at Edwyn.

"Well – what's the matter? You too good for beans and bread?"

"No....no.....ma'am. They're...fi.......fine."

"They're fi.....fi....fine. Stop your stuttering, boy. Damn. More and more like your father," she complained as she walked outside to light another cigarette.

When she was gone, Tristan reached over and poured Edwyn's beans into his plate and dared him to say anything. Edwyn didn't say a word. He didn't like beans that much anyway and he thought he saw something crawling in them. He simply ate his bread and drank the water and got up from the table. He went to the bedroom and got into his bed and thought about the puppy and the story he and Caleb had begun to read. In a few minutes, Tristan came and sat down on the edge of the bed and asked Edwyn again where he had been all day.

"Just...out.... In the woods. Looking a...a...aaround."

"Did you find anything while you were looking ahhhhhh..round?"

"No."

He knew better than to tell Tristan about the puppy or the cabin. He wasn't sure what he would do, but he understood it wouldn't be good.

The next day their mother told them she was too tired to do any book reading and they could have the day to themselves, so Edwyn hurried out and started heading back to the cabin. He knew Tristan would try and follow him, so he went back and forth, up and down the mountain until Tristan believed he was lost and decided he should try and find his way back home. Edwyn smiled as he watched him walk away and smiled even bigger when he knocked on the door and saw Caleb waiting for him.

"Pup is doing fine, Edwyn. Waiting on you to feed him. By the way, I made some extra biscuits this morning that I'm not going to eat. Would you like some milk and some biscuits?"

"Yes, sir. I would li....like that very..mu...much."

"Good. You eat first, then you feed that pup, and then we'll start back on that book. You remember the name of the story, don't you?"

"Yes sir. 'Rip Van Winkle,'" he answered as he remembered the bell.

"That's wonderful, Edwyn. Wonderful," Caleb said as he smiled and took a drink from the glass jar that they drank from yesterday. "Whew...that water's got a bite to it this morning!"

By the end of the day, they had finished the story, fed the pup three times, had lunch of honey and biscuits and milk, and Caleb had drunk half that jar of water. Edwyn noticed the water smelled different than it did yesterday and asked Caleb if he was sure it was okay.

"Well, Edwyn, if you can keep a secret and I think you can, this isn't just water in this jar. It's got water in it but I put some other stuff in it too that makes it, uh...a stronger drink. A drink for old folks like me. I call it rheumatism medicine. Helps grease these old joints so that they don't creak and ache so much."

"Oh," Edwyn replied. "I d...d..don't need that yet, do I?"

"No, Edwyn. It's not for young folks. Just older folks like me. But more importantly than this medicine I've been drinking - what did you think of the story?"

"I li...liked it. Are there re...re...really lit...lit...tle men li..like that in the woods?"

"I haven't seen any yet, but that don't mean there aren't any. Could be all sorts of things in these woods that none of us seen, but that's what's fun about these books. It makes you think about what may be, even if no one but Mr. Irving seen it. And he may have only seen it in his mind. Just imagined it happened. Do you understand what that means?"

"Yes sir. I i...i...imagine things too...I i...i...imagine my father co...co...coming home soon. And I i..i..imagine that pup get...getting bigger. Is that goo...good imagine?"

"The word you want to say is imagination, not imagine, but you're right. Those are good things to imagine. If this keeps up, you may become quite the reader and I'd say in about three or four more weeks, that pup of yours will be ready to get up and go for a little walk."

Edwyn grinned and even laughed at the thought of walking in the woods with that little dog. He thanked Caleb for the food and said he would see him tomorrow. When he got home, his mother was waiting on him at the front door with Tristan and she told him to come in and sit down.

"Where you been going to, Edwyn? You find something that might help us? What's that I smell on your breath? Smells like honey. Did you find some honey? We could use some honey for our bread. Don't hold back on your momma now, boy."

Edwyn didn't know what to say but he knew it would be best if he could keep both of them from finding Caleb and the dog.

"Yes, I f...f...found some honey. I co...could get you...so...some. If you...g..g..give me a jar...I'll get it.... to...tomorrow..."

"Well take your brother with you. Don't want something happening to you and then no one else knows where the honey is."

Edwyn knew he had to think fast.

"I c..c..can't do....do that. I met a man....in th..the forest....He has the huh...huh..honey but he....told me..... that no one else c..c..could come....by.. He k...k...keeps....things....hidden...with....jars....of......"

"Damn, boy! You done come up on some moonshiner. Hellfire, you're lucky you ain't dead. He musta taken a liking to you. And you're right. They don't like other folks coming by. Tell you this - I'll keep Tristan from following you, but you bring back some honey and some of that shine to me. You got that?"

"Shi....ne?"

"Yeah, boy. He'll know what I mean. You do that and I'll make you some good biscuits and honey and beans."

"Yes, ma'am."

"You hungry? You want some beans and bread?"

"No, ma'am. I'll just g...g...go to bed if that's o....okay."

"Yes. That's okay. C'mon, Tristan. I'll fix you some beans and bread and then off to bed with you too. Gonna be a good day tomorrow."

Tristan sneered at his brother as he watched him go to their room. He didn't like that Edwyn knew something that he didn't and that his mother was now being nice to his stupid brother. That night when he went into their room, he walked over and punched Edwyn in the stomach, knocking the breath out of him.

"Expect that every night that you don't show me where that honey is," Tristan declared, but Edwyn didn't care. He could take a punch in the stomach every night knowing his pup would be okay.

Edwyn saw Tristan try and follow him again the next day, but was able to lose him as he moved through the woods like a fox. When he arrived at Caleb's cabin, he explained everything to him. Caleb smiled and said that he would be happy to give him the "shine" and a jar of honey if that kept his mother away. Edwyn thanked him and that day, after feeding the pup, they began reading "The Legend of Sleepy Hollow." Caleb warned him before they started reading that there were ghosts in the story and from Edywn's confused look, he knew he had to explain what the word ghost meant.

"Is that part of M...Mmmm....Mister Ir....Irving's im...imagine... im..imagination too? Like the....little men?"

Caleb chuckled and nodded his head.

"What a very smart question and yes, it is. Mr. Irving had a very good imagination."

"Have you ever seen a g...g..ghost?"

And just like the answer he had for the little men in the forest, Caleb replied in the same way.

"No, I haven't, but that doesn't mean there aren't any," he said as he laughed and took a drink of his funny-smelling water.

Over the next several months, Caleb supplied Edwyn with honey and the occasional jar of "shine" and Caleb's mother was happier than she had been in a long time. In addition to the moonshine, she had also started receiving a monthly check from the Navy. She bought just enough food so that they wouldn't starve and spent the rest on nice clothes and beauty items for herself.

The way his mother felt over Edwyn's "gifts" enraged Tristan and he swore he would find out where he was getting the jars that he brought home every two or three days.

By this time, the pup was up and moving about and he loved going on walks with Edwyn and Caleb. As they were walking along a trail one day, Caleb told him he needed to give the pup a name. Edwyn looked up in the sky and was reminded of something he had read in the "Rip Van Winkle" story. He asked Caleb if those skies were "azure," remembering what Caleb had said about being cold and shaking and saying, "brrrr" and then telling him to leave off the "b" as they said that word several times.

Caleb laughed loudly. "By George, those are azure skies, Edwyn! Azure skies with clouds that look like big scoops of vanilla ice cream, don't you think?"

"Yes," Edwyn replied. It had been a long time since he had vanilla ice cream but the thought of it made him smile.

Without any warning, Edwyn saw his brother standing there, glaring at him, with rocks in his hand.

"I knew I'd find you sooner or later," he said as he threw a rock as hard as he could and hit Edwyn in the head, knocking him to the ground. He then heard a whelp as the next rocks hit the pup's body. Just before he closed his eyes, he heard Caleb's thundering voice and saw the clouds had now turned deep purple and blue.

When Edwyn awoke, he was lying on the couch in Caleb's cabin with a cool, wet bandage around his head. He felt dizzy as he looked over at the pup on the rug with a bandage around his chest. The rag was bloody and he tried to get up and go to him, but he felt like he was going to be sick. He fell back onto the couch and though he tried to fight it, he could not, and closed his eyes and was soon asleep.

He didn't know how long he had been on the couch but when he woke up again, Caleb was sitting next to him, and there was a large gray dog beside Caleb.

"What happened?" Edwyn asked. "Where is the puppy?"

"He's right here, Edwyn. He's not a puppy anymore. He's fully grown. Been watching over you for some time now. He won't let anyone but me come near you. I thought you and him were both goners until your brother saw me and knew he needed to leave. I'm not sure what I would have done to him if he hadn't. You and this dog of yours have taken quite a time to heal. Your dad is home from the war now. But I need to warn you, he doesn't look the same."

"How...?"

"I know, Edwyn. It's not easy to understand. But you've been asleep for a while. What people would call a coma. That's just a word that means your brain needed to rest so it could heal. It's taken some time, but just like your father, you are strong."

"Is my father okay?"

"He will be. You should go and see him. And take Gray with you."

"Gray?"

"Your dog. I had to name him. I thought he looked like a big gray cloud. What do you think?"

"I agree Caleb. A great big cloud." Gray leaned over and licked Edwyn's hand.

"Will you come with me? To see my father and family? I want to tell them how you saved me and Gray."

"I can't, Edwyn. I'm afraid I don't have much longer on this earth. But that's okay. Like I told you some time ago, I'm old but I have lots of good memories. Just remember to be strong. Your father would want you to do that and sometimes that means that you have to learn to forgive and forget the past. You and your father will both need to do that."

"I don't understand," Edwyn said.

"You will. Now, you and Gray go on home. Your father is waiting for you."

Edwyn got up and hugged Caleb and Gray whined as he did so. Caleb handed him a leather pouch and told him it was some money that he had saved from selling his special water and that it would help him and his family make a new start. Edwyn thanked him and started his walk home with Gray by his side. Gray's head was now up to Edwyn's shoulders and he looked like two dogs instead of one. As he neared his house, he saw his brother sitting on the porch, but he looked different. He was now taller than their mother and he looked even meaner.

When Tristan saw his brother walking toward him with Gray, he stood up and almost fell backward. He yelled out to his mother to come and see what was coming their way. His mother ambled outside and threw her cigarette on the ground as she shook her head.

"I thought you told me he was dead! Fell off the side of a mountain! Isn't that what you said, Tristan?"

Tristan didn't reply and the memory came rushing back to Edwyn. He remembered his brother throwing rocks at him and his dog and knew why he wasn't replying to their mother's question.

"Hell, where have you been, boy, for the past three years? Shit, your damn father, or what used to be your father, has come home. He looks like a monster if you ask me. How in the hell he expects us to make a living with those burns on his face and arm and leg, I have no idea. But shit, he ain't worried about none of that. Not surprising. He ain't never been worried about a god damn thing."

Edwyn recognized the man walking out of the house even though his face was horribly burned. But Edwyn didn't see a burned face, just his father, smiling and happy to see him. He could feel the tears welling up in his eyes.

"Hel....lo...Ed......Edwyn. I've......miss..missed you....so..mu...much."

As Edwyn ran toward his father and wrapped his arms around him, he dropped the leather pouch on the porch. Tristan quickly picked it up as he eyed the large gray dog that had now approached the porch and started to growl. Even so, Tristan opened the pouch and pulled out several of the gold coins.

"I'll be damned. Let me see those!" his mother said and grabbed the coins from Tristan's hand.

Just as she did, Gray sprang up and sunk his teeth into Tristan's wrist, dragging him to the ground.

"Mom! Help me! This dog, he's hurting me! He's going to tear my hand off!"

"I'll help you," his mother said as she snatched the pouch from his hand and ran away. Gray released Tristan's wrist and looked over at

Edwyn once before running after his mother. Though they could not see what happened, they all heard a scream and then silence. Within a few moments, Gray came trotting back toward the house. His muzzle dripped with blood.

"Tris...tan. Are....you okay?" his father asked.

Tristan nodded his head as fourteen years of tears flowed down his dirty face like rain making gullies in the side of a hill.

"Where did you get those co...coins?" his father asked Edwyn.

"I've been in a coma, Dad. Caleb helped me. I ummm... I stumbled. Yeah. I fell over a tree root in the woods and hit my head on a rock. He helped me get better and raise my dog. He said you knew him."

"Yes. He was.....my...uncle and a good man.   He was a moon..shi...shiner. Liked...go....gold....coins. He...taught me how to read and help....helped me with my spe...speech."

His father started to stagger and Edwyn caught him and asked Tristan for his help. Together they settled him into the rocking chair on the front porch.

Both his sons could see the tears in their father's eyes and were unsure what to say.

"Caleb did...didn't get ahhh..along with your mother. He never came by here. He stay...stayed to himself. But I saw him. I saw him... ju....just before he died and I enlisted in the war."

Edwyn's face turned cloud-white, as if all the blood had drained from it into his feet. He felt like he was going to faint but Tristan steadied him within his arms.

"How long...How long ... did she say it has been?"

"Three years. You've been gone three years, Edwyn. I am sorry. I am so very, very sorry, brother."

Gray came over and licked both Tristan and Edwyn's hands and laid down beside Edwyn.

His father asked him how his dog got its name and Edwyn said the words without even realizing what he was saying. He then remembered the name of Rip Van Winkle's dog and heard his father say that was a good name for his dog, considering it was a wolf.

The Willful Child

Once upon a time, there was a child who was willful and did not do what his mother wanted. For this reason, God was displeased with him and caused him to become ill, and no doctor could help him, and in a short time, he lay on his deathbed.

He was lowered into a grave and covered with earth, but his little arm suddenly came forth and reached up, and it didn't help when they put it back in and put fresh earth over it, for the little arm always came out again. So the mother herself had to go to the grave and beat the little arm with a switch, and as soon as she had done that, it withdrew, and the child finally came to rest beneath the earth.

Hair Follicles

Once upon a time, there was a mother who loved her daughter more than anything else in the world. She felt she had been blessed beyond her wildest imagination at the time of her birth, even though the father abandoned her as soon as he learned she planned to have the baby. She had been scared at first, but the moment she held the little girl in her arms her fears disappeared like a blanket of morning dew pulled away from the tops of the flowers and plants by the warm and lighthearted sun.

She had never felt this brave before her baby's birth. For many years she had battled with insecurity because she suffered from recurrent bouts of alopecia. But, even with the disease, she was a beautiful girl, and the steroid creams, pills, and injections had worked each time and encouraged her hair to grow back. Nevertheless, the concern that she would lose her hair and she would run out of possible cures always lingered in the back of her mind and frightened her.

The first seven years of her life would be considered by anyone as heavenly and as beautiful as the gardens that grew around her home. Her father was a botanist and if you knew nothing else about him besides his profession you would have reasoned that was why he named his daughter Laurel. But she was named after her mother who died from complications during childbirth. One might also believe that Laurel might have been haunted by the death of her mother once she realized the origin of her name, but her father was devoted to her and she understood she was loved by him and he made sure Laurel knew what a wonderful person her mother had been. With her father's devotion and with that knowledge of her mother, Laurel never felt regret, only honor and pride to be named for her.

Her father involved Laurel in all his work, taking her around the world to study different types of plants. She loved every moment with him and learning about the diverse world that grew around them. She also came to know that her mother had been an avid gardener too. She began to realize that as she grew up with her flourishing interests in plants, she was developing into a living tribute to her mother, which made her very happy, both professionally and personally.

She had just completed her master's degree in Botany and Plant Pathology and was beginning work on her doctorate when her father died of a stroke while working in their garden. Laurel was sad and would miss her father every day, but she was comforted that he died doing something he loved. She became pregnant soon after his death and when she held her baby in her arms, she knew immediately how to honor both of her parents. The baby's name would be Fleur, the French word for flower. At that moment, in her opinion, there was not a prettier flower in the entire world.

Laurel inherited her father's house and the gardens kept the memories of him fresh in her mind, and also connected her to her mother. Just as her father had done, Laurel made sure Fleur was involved from a very early age in tending the garden and learning about the many plants that grew there. When Fleur turned eight, Laurel began to notice that her alopecia was returning. Even though she used steroids in every form and tried topical immunotherapy, she could not halt the progression of the disease. In fact, her doctor told her he was afraid that she would soon be bald.

When she found her mother crying the day she learned of the news from the doctor, Fleur asked her what was wrong. Laurel explained she was losing her hair but that she shouldn't be worried. She reassured her daughter that she wasn't dying and would be fine. She was just having a "moment to feel sorry for myself" but she would get over it and everything would be okay.

Fleur looked at her mother and told her that she would be pretty without hair and Laurel cried even more. What she heard next from her daughter almost stopped her breath. Fleur told her mother she could have her hair.

Fleur's hair had never been cut from the time she was born. She had beautiful auburn hair that hung down below her waist. As Laurel hugged her daughter and looked at her hair, she began to wonder if there was some type of gene that enabled her daughter's hair to grow in such an abundant, almost abnormal manner. *How ironic and wonderful if that gene truly existed,* she thought considering the genetic mutation that was believed to be the cause of her disease. And as if Fleur could understand what her mother was thinking, she gazed up at her and told her that they could cut away all of her hair and it wouldn't bother her.

"Mine will grow back, Mommy, and when you wear my hair we will look like sisters," Fleur said with a smile. When her daughter first made the suggestion, Laurel thought she was just being sweet and loving. But the more she looked at her daughter's hair, the more she realized what she was suggesting was indeed a possibility.

So, the next day, Laurel took her daughter to a hair loss center and told them what Fleur wanted to do for her. The women who worked there were moved by the gesture. When they explained to Fleur that they would need to cut off all of her hair to get the amount necessary for a wig, Fleur told them the same thing she had told her mother, adding this time, "It will just make me look like Mommy now and then later when the wig is finished, we will look the same again." When she heard these words, Laurel knew she was truly blessed.

Eight weeks later, Laurel's wig was ready and Fleur's hair had already started to grow back. When Laurel put the wig on and looked in the mirror, she couldn't believe what she saw.

"See, Mommy; I told you. We look like twins!" Everyone in the store clapped and cried at the same time. Though they didn't look like twins, Laurel did notice how the hair made her and Fleur look much more related. *Funny how just a little hair makes such a difference.* Laurel smiled as she hugged her daughter and whispered, "Thank you." On the way home, they stopped for Fleur's favorite pizza and then got some cupcakes from a bakery she loved. It was a wonderful day and one Laurel told her daughter she would never forget. Fleur told her mother the very same thing.

The next morning, Laurel felt different when she put on the wig. Her insecurity was gone and she even seemed to have more energy. *Amazing what a little vanity will do for you,* she thought to herself and laughed as she prepared Fleur's breakfast and got her ready for school.

"After school, I'll bring you to my lab and we can work with some new exotic plants we got from Texas. Something is destroying the Beach Morning Glory which is a real problem because it helps stabilize the sand dunes there on the coast. You will love them, Fleur. They are beautiful vines with flowers; some are white and yellow, and some are a deep pink color that people often refer to as fuchsia."

"They sound beautiful, Mommy. What's wrong with them?"

"I'm not sure. They just aren't thriving and growing well. I suspect it may be pollution of some sort, but we will examine them and see. After we figure it out, I think a trip to the coast of Texas might be in order – just to make sure we have resolved the issue. Maybe over spring break?"

"Sounds wonderful to me, Mommy. I've never been to Texas."

"That is correct, young lady, but we'll fix that problem in a month or so," Laurel said as she tickled Fleur and they both laughed.

Laurel discovered what the plant problem was after several days of analysis. A microscopic fungal saprophyte was destroying them. Laurel made sure to show it to Fleur. As Fleur examined the fungus under the microscope, Laurel explained to her what she was looking at and then asked her a question.

"Do you remember what I said a saprophyte was?"

Fleur was very smart and responded as she always did; in an almost robotic fashion with the correct answer.

"A saprophyte is a plant, fungus, or microorganism that lives on dead or decaying organic matter."

"Excellent, Fleur! Usually, by doing what they do, the soil is enriched. But it seems like this particular species is actually killing the vine. Perhaps it just doesn't separate the dead organic matter from the living. That would be very unique, but we will figure it out!" Laurel said as she took her daughter into her arms and twirled her around several times.

Over the next month, Laurel developed an organic fungicide that not only destroyed the fungus after a certain amount of time but also provided a soil that energized and promoted the growth of new flowers and enabled the Beach Morning Glory to flourish once again. During spring break, Laurel and Fleur visited Texas, just as she had promised, and they saw how well the cure worked in the natural environment. They spent the rest of the week visiting different places in Texas. They drove well over a thousand miles, and Laurel was constantly surprised by how much energy she had now. She was certain it was due to Fleur because she believed the love she shared with her was empowering.

Even when they returned to their daily routines back in Oregon, nothing seemed routine anymore. Laurel attributed it all to Fleur. With each passing day, she felt more connected to her daughter. Laurel knew the compliments from an adoring daughter and their consistent interactions were the elements driving that psycho-social attachment, but she couldn't help but feel as if there was something physical too. *I hope my father felt this way about me,* Laurel thought and smiled.

Soon after Fleur turned thirteen, Laurel noticed a distinct difference in her daughter. She had helped her through her first menstrual cycle and had explained to her the hormonal changes that were occurring in her body, but she could tell something else was still bothering her daughter. She didn't want to broach the subject of sex with her now, considering she was only thirteen, but she knew she should sit down and explain everything to her so she would not make a mistake she regretted.

She was amazed at how interested Fleur was in the science of reproduction and she asked her mother many questions about it. She even asked if they could examine the process anatomically on the internet and Laurel agreed, ensuring what they viewed was purely biological in nature. *Well, at least she understands everything and knows the issues,* Laurel thought. *She will be fine. I raised her well, so that is all I can do for now. Plus, Fleur knows I will always be there for her,* she reminded herself as she went to sleep that night.

Laurel was right about her daughter. She raised her well and she did not need to worry about an unexpected and unplanned pregnancy. But she also knew when her daughter turned seventeen that Fleur would not live to see her eighteenth birthday. All the energy Laurel once had was diminishing each day and she began to find it difficult to even focus. It was in that year, just before she died, that Laurel remembered being told by the nursing staff that her baby had died in utero. But yet, twenty minutes later, she had delivered a healthy baby that day.

The doctors had not been able to explain it and Laurel didn't care or investigate any further as to how this was possible though she knew by not doing so, she was ignoring the world of science in which she dwelled. For seventeen years she had convinced herself it had just been some sort of miracle, as she had refused to acknowledge the truth. But she couldn't ignore the truth any longer. She now understood that the new unexplained energy which had enveloped every aspect of her body had indeed come from her daughter, except it was not simply due to the "aura" of maternal love. It was because of her daughter's hair that she had worn every day for the past nine years. In the beginning, the hair was a conduit and provided her energy, but now it was killing her. She knew her daughter was some form of saprophyte, unlike anything of this world. That is why Laurel had been taking small doses of arsenic over the past year, knowing that the poisonous substance would settle within the hair follicles like silt in a riverbed, and go undetected until it was too late. She had sensed when her daughter turned eighteen the incubation period would be over and she could not release this unknown threat into the environment.

During the graveside service, Fleur reached out to her biological parents telepathically and told them that she was ready to begin the next phase of the experiment, just as she began to cough. *That was odd,* she thought. She had never been sick a day in her entire life. But as she continued to cough, a sharp pain surged through her body and she realized she could not breathe. She fell over dead at the funeral of her mother. Those who were there said she died of a broken heart. They were right. Although if an autopsy had been performed, they would have learned that she died of three broken hearts, or from a scientific perspective; she died of severe cardiomyopathy from arsenic poisoning within the three hearts that were normal for her particular species.

Clever Gretel

Once upon a time, there was a cook whose name was Gretel. She wore shoes with red heels, and whenever she went out wearing them she would turn this way and that way, and she was very cheerful, thinking, "You are a beautiful girl!"

Then after returning home, because she was so happy, she would drink a swallow of wine, and the wine would give her an appetite, so she would taste the best of what she had cooked until she was quite full, and then she would say, "The cook has to know how the food tastes."

One day her master said to her, "Gretel, this evening a guest is coming. Prepare two chickens for me, the best way that you can."

"Yes indeed, sir," answered Gretel. She killed the chickens, scalded them, plucked them, stuck them on the spit, and then, as evening approached, put them over the fire to roast. The chickens began to brown and were nearly done, but the guest had not yet arrived.

Gretel called to her master, "If the guest doesn't come, I'll have to take the chickens from the fire. And it will be a crying shame if they're not eaten soon because they're at their juicy best right now."

The master answered, "You're right. I'll run and fetch the guest myself."

As soon as the master had turned his back, Gretel set the spit and the chickens aside and thought, "Standing here by the fire has made me sweaty and thirsty. Who knows when they will be back? Meanwhile, I'll just run down into the cellar and take a swallow."

So she ran down, lifted a jug to her lips, saying, "God bless it for you, Gretel!" and took a healthy drink. "Wine belongs together," she said further. "It's not good to keep it apart," and took another healthy drink.

Then she went and placed the chickens over the fire again, basted them with butter, and cheerfully turned the spit. Because the roasting chickens smelled so good, she thought, "They could be lacking something. I'd better taste them!" She tested them with her fingers, and said, "My, these chickens are good! It's a sin and a shame that they won't be eaten at once!"

She ran to the window to see if her master and his guest were arriving, but she saw no one. Returning to the chickens, she said, "That one wing is burning. I'd better just eat it." So she cut it off and ate it, and it tasted very good. When she had finished it, she thought, "I'd better eat the other one too, or the master will see that something is missing."

When both wings had been eaten, she once again looked for her master, but could not see him. Then it occurred to her, "Who knows? Perhaps they've gone somewhere else to eat and aren't coming here at all." Then she said, "Well, Gretel, be of good cheer! The one has already been cut into. Have another drink and eat the rest of it. When it's gone, you can relax. Why should this good gift of God go to waste?"

So she ran to the cellar once again, downed a noble drink, and cheerfully finished off the first chicken. When the one chicken was gone, and her master still had not yet returned, she looked at the other chicken and said, "Where the one is, the other should follow.

108

The two belong together. What is right for the one, can't be wrong for the other. I believe that if I have another drink, it will do me no harm." So, she took another hearty drink and sent the second chicken running after the first one.

Just as she was making the most of it, her master returned, calling out, "Gretel, hurry up, the guest is right behind me."

"Yes, sir, I'm getting it ready," answered Gretel.

Meanwhile, the master saw that the table was set, and he picked up the large knife that he wanted to carve the chickens with and stood in the hallway sharpening it.

The guest arrived and knocked politely on the door. Gretel ran to see who it was, and when she saw that it was the guest, she held a finger before her mouth, and said, "Be quiet! Be quiet! Hurry and get away from here. If my master catches you, you'll be sorry. Yes, he invited you for an evening meal, but all he really wants is to cut off both of your ears. Listen, he's sharpening his knife for it right now."

The guest heard the whetting and ran back down the steps as fast as he could.

Then Gretel, who was not a bit lazy, ran to her master, crying, "Just what kind of a guest did you invite?"

"Why, Gretel? What do you mean by that?"

"Well," she said, "he took both of the chickens off the platter, just as I was about to carry them out, and then ran away with them."

"Now that's a fine tune!" said the master, feeling sorry about the loss of the good chickens. "At the least, he could have left one of them, so I would have something to eat."

He called out to him to stop, but the guest pretended not to hear. Then he ran after him, the knife still in his hand, shouting, "Just one! Just one!" But the guest could only think that he wanted him to give up one of his ears, so he ran as though there was a fire burning beneath him, in order to get home with both ears.

The Games Cornish Hens Play

Once upon a time, there was a woman who had learned to become an excellent cook. Her friends would call her a "gourmet" even though she had no formal culinary training. No, her skills were born within the kitchens of her mother and grandmother (who were both considered very good cooks) and as she grew older, she devoured every moment she spent with them learning their recipes. Like her mother and grandmother, this woman loved to drink wine when she cooked, but unlike her teachers, she began to love the wine more than the cooking and because of this, developed many health problems.

She had so many health problems, she was becoming a risk to herself. Upon advice from her best friend, her husband agreed it was time to act, and they engaged in an intervention. From that point forward, she was placed into rehabilitation clinics on more than one occasion. Each time she entered a clinic, she did well and would be discharged into the care of her husband. And each time she left a clinic, she promised her husband that she would not allow this problem to recur, but she was mentally and physically unable to fulfill those promises.

It was a subtle insecurity at first. Saying goodbye to her husband and best friend as she went into the clinic brought tears and hugs that lingered on her face and in her arms, long after they were gone. If she had ever been asked, she would never have been able to tell anyone when the jealous thoughts first crept into her mind. But there they were, moving through her neurons like cockroaches that scurried amidst the shadows and crevices of a dark kitchen.

Soon the roaches became rats, and the obvious symbolism filled her nostrils with a cynical and foul aroma. When she was alone each day in the clinic, in what was supposed to be a place of healing, she only thought of how she was being wronged, rather than how she was being helped. Perhaps she had a proclivity for these thoughts before she became ill. Perhaps her illness only encouraged these thoughts to surface; repressed by a strong mind, but weakened by one that was soaked in alcohol. Perhaps they were created as a byproduct of elevated enzymes that began to poison her mind as well as her body. No one would ever know for sure. The only certainty was that they became an obsession that could not be controlled.

She was not foolish enough to allow these thoughts to betray her while inside the facility or whenever she was released back home. She knew she could not share these feelings with anyone until she had firm evidence that a betrayal was occurring. She understood she would just be labeled delusional and paranoid. She believed she had already suffered sufficient indignity and she would not allow those words to be added to the medical chart of her delicate and suffering persona. She knew she had been wronged and was now forced to seek relief and absolution elsewhere. She would prove it and then show everyone how blind they had been to the root of her problems.

She became quite adept at following her husband or friend without their knowledge, but she could never catch either of them doing anything wrong. There was no physical evidence of them sleeping together. However, there were multiple occasions when they met in a restaurant or coffee shop and spent time together and she knew what that meant. They were devising a plan to get rid of her for good and they would most likely have her committed for life so that they could be together forever without judgment by anyone.

Each time she saw them together, she became more enraged at their dishonesty and lies. The conspiring nature of the two most important people in her life, consumed her every thought. If she could not catch them having sex, she would have to catch them in a lie. Her husband and best friend thought it odd when she began asking them a myriad of unconnected questions, but she could tell by the expressions on their faces that she was getting close to them saying the "wrong thing." Their words of encouragement and love were simply a way to misdirect her thinking and she would have none of it.

They hope I won't get well, she thought. *They want to dump my body into the well and be done with me, but that won't happen. Those nice words are exactly what my best friend and husband who are having an affair would say.*

112

She began keeping a diary of their encouraging remarks and she recognized there were keywords present in those comments that would reveal their scheming and deceit if she could only fit everything together. And with each passing day and every word she recorded, she heard a voice in her head telling her that with a drink of wine, she could probably put together all the puzzle pieces that sat there on the paper, defying her to figure out what they meant. Several times she resisted that voice, but it was an unfair battle with a predictable outcome. She would start drinking again and become so ill that she would have to be readmitted to the rehabilitation clinic, tormented and frustrated that she could not discern the answers she needed.

During her latest admission to the clinic, she realized that she had access to some very intelligent people who had probably seen and heard everything before and could possibly help her unmask her husband's infidelity. She just had to be careful not to let the therapist or nurses know what she planned to do to the two individuals once she had uncovered their plot. If they learned that she intended to kill her husband and best friend when she gathered all the necessary evidence, she would never be allowed to leave the institution in which she was confined.

Clever girl, she told herself as she sat in her room and pretended to read. *Think. How will you get the therapist to help you? What questions do you need to ask without giving away your true thoughts? You need to think like them; those on the outside who are designing and planning their lives once you're dead, and those here on the inside who think your illness is your own fault. I know, I know. Yes, that will work,* she decided and she memorized all the questions she would need.

At the required therapy sessions, she heard the clinical psychologist and the physician tell her that if she continued to drink, she would be dead in less than a year. That's when she realized she couldn't trust anyone in there either. *They are being paid to say all of this by them. It just makes it easier for them to make my death look like an accident. But I have a plan. Dinner. Dinner with the three of us. That will reveal the truth,* she thought and listened to the words of the doctors and nodded that she understood what was being said.

A month later, she was released and her husband and best friend were there waiting for her. The doctors had informed them of the seriousness of her disease state and they were less than hopeful she could change at this point. They were ready for the worst and were surprised by the upbeat manner in which she greeted them that day.

She looked like her old self again, they both thought. She was engaged in the conversation, interested in the world, and told them she wanted to get back in the kitchen and celebrate. As soon as they heard the word celebrate, her husband and best friend looked at each other and she just smiled when she noticed their discreet glance. *The trap is set,* she thought and she laughed as she told them not to worry; when she said "celebrate," she didn't mean with wine. She just wanted to cook a nice dinner for both of them and celebrate the first day of her "new life."

They had never heard her say that before in all the many times they had gone through this process and they both said in unison, "That's wonderful!" She smiled, even though beneath that smile her teeth were gritted. *Shit. This is nauseating. Now they even say the same thing at the same time. This is going to be so easy and so very gratifying.*

She asked her husband to stop at the grocery store so she could get the ingredients for dinner. Within ten minutes she returned, holding up some shopping bags and shuffling them around. "See – you didn't have to worry - no clinking of glass!" she said in a boisterous and happy manner.

Once they were home, she announced that she wanted a little rest before starting dinner. She would have everything ready by 7:00 p.m. but neither of them could be there while she cooked because she wanted it to be a surprise. She kissed her husband on the forehead and her best friend on the cheek and said she would see them later that evening.

In the bedroom, she stood next to the closed door and listened to them talking. Her best friend was telling her husband that she shouldn't be left alone and her husband replied that he thought it would be okay. There was no wine or alcohol of any kind in the house and he would make sure she didn't have access to the car keys to go anywhere before he left for the afternoon. She heard her friend reluctantly agree as they walked downstairs.

Before she got in bed, she walked over and looked out her window. Garden therapy had been proposed by one of the nurses the last time she had been discharged from the rehab center. She had planted four small cherry trees and lots of flowers and she wondered how those

114

plants were doing. The trees and flowers were flourishing and she smiled as she lay down and thought about the menu and how she would have her revenge that evening.

At exactly 4:30 p.m., she came downstairs and her husband said he hadn't seen her look so happy in a long time. She replied that she was feeling wonderful but that he needed to leave now and return with her best friend "in tow" at 7 p.m., sharp. He said that would be great and that he was looking forward to it as he kissed her on the cheek. As soon as she was sure he was gone, she walked into the backyard and dug up each of the four trees she had planted. At the base of each tree was a bottle of wine and she gathered them up and walked back into the house.

She cleaned off the bottles, uncorked one, poured herself a glass, and began cooking. She was making Cornish game hens with a shallot and truffle gravy, glazed carrots, scalloped potatoes, and for dessert, key lime tarts. She had made this dinner at least a dozen times and knew it would be the perfect meal to mask her true intent, as they would be preoccupied with the wonderful tastes on their palate.

By 6:30 p.m., the food was cooked and she had finished off three and one-half of the four bottles. Because of her damaged liver, she was beyond intoxicated, though she believed she had everything under control. After placing everything on the table, she sat down and poured another glass of wine. She began to think about how she would start the conversation when she saw one of the Cornish game hens stand up and start talking.

"You do realize that those two you plan to trap tonight have been alone with each other for over two hours. I don't have to tell you what they have been doing, do I?"

Before she could answer, another hen stood up and poked its wing into the breast of its companion, and began laughing.

"Well, they aren't doing as much talking as they are moaning and groaning!" it said, and then she saw all of the Cornish hens stand up and laugh. Two of them began skipping around the table and singing a rhyme.

"Hubby and bestie, doing the nastee, Hubby and bestie, doing the nastee..."

"Shut up!" she yelled.

"You shut up, you damn drunk!" they all yelled back at her and one of them walked over and stood right in front of her face.

115

"You stupid fool! You never planned anything but this dinner. You have no idea how to trick them into confessing that they are having an affair! You are too drunk to even have a conversation unless they both have a degree in slurred words."

"Shut up, you damn chicken! You don't know anything."

"I know we aren't chickens," it said and they all laughed at her even more.

She thought she was going to go mad if she continued to listen to them. That's when she realized how to make the noise stop. She picked up two knives and jammed them into her eardrums. She almost fainted from the pain, but she pulled her head up and yelled at the hens.

Though she knew what she yelled, she couldn't hear her words and could no longer hear the hens that were now staring at her. Triumphantly, she laughed and took another drink of wine. She then saw one of the hens take a piece of bread and begin doing something obscene with it. She saw the other three clapping their wings together as they pointed at the overt sexual innuendo and then over at her. She knew they were mocking her and she wouldn't have any of it. She grabbed two more knives and stuck them into her eyes. As her head fell toward the table, the knives were driven further into her head and immediately impaired her ability to think or remember anything, which for her sake, was an act of compassion. Her ill body revolted because of the intense pain and copious amounts of wine that coursed through her body, and she vomited blood and wine numerous times.

Because of her cirrhotic liver, her ability to form a blood clot was lacking and she had begun to bleed to death as soon as she incurred the first injury. Her husband and best friend called for help when they arrived, but there was nothing anyone could do and she died thirty minutes after arriving at the hospital.

The psychologist and physician were right. It took less than a year for her to die once she started drinking again. No one could convince her that they were not having an affair, but the husband and best friend had convinced everyone else. So, the fact that they started seeing each other a month after she was buried didn't seem inappropriate. Everyone simply viewed the relationship as a natural progression of events considering the pain the two of them had endured and the solace that they both now needed and found within each other's company.

The Girl without Hands

A miller fell slowly but surely into poverty until finally, he had nothing more than his mill and a large apple tree that stood behind it. One day he had gone into the forest to gather wood, where he was approached by an old man, whom he had never seen before, and who said, "Why do you torment yourself with chopping wood? I will make you rich if you will promise me that which is standing behind your mill."

"What can that be but my apple tree?" thought the miller, said yes, and signed it over to the strange man.

The latter, however, laughed mockingly and said, "I will come in three years and get what belongs to me," then went away.

When he arrived home, his wife came up to him and said, "Miller, tell me, where did all the wealth come from that is suddenly in our house? All at once all the chests and boxes are full, and no one brought it here, and I don't know where it came from."

He answered, "It comes from a strange man whom I met in the woods and who promised me great treasures if I would but sign over to him that which stands behind the mill. We can give up the large apple tree for all this."

"Oh, husband!" said the woman, terrified. "That was the devil. He didn't mean the apple tree, but our daughter, who was just then standing behind the mill sweeping the yard."

The miller's daughter was a beautiful and pious girl, and she lived the three years worshipping God and without sin. When the time was up and the day came when the evil one was to get her, she washed herself clean and drew a circle around herself with chalk. The devil appeared very early in the morning, but he could not approach her.

He spoke angrily to the miller, "Keep water away from her, so she cannot wash herself anymore. Otherwise, I have no power over her."

The miller was frightened and did what he was told. The next morning the devil returned, but she had wept into her hands, and they were entirely clean.

Thus, he still could not approach her, and he spoke angrily to the miller, "Chop off her hands. Otherwise, I cannot get to her."

The miller was horrified and answered, "How could I chop off my own child's hands?"

Then the evil one threatened him, saying, "If you do not do it, then you will be mine, and I will take you yourself."

This frightened the father, and he promised to obey him. Then he went to the girl and said, "My child, if I do not chop off both of your hands, then the devil will take me away, and in my fear, I have promised him to do this. Help me in my need, and forgive me of the evil that I am going to do to you."

She answered, "Dear father, do with me what you will. I am your child," and with that, she stretched forth both hands and let her father chop them off.

The devil came a third time, but she had wept so long and so much onto the stumps, that they were entirely clean. Then he had to give up, for he had lost all claim to her.

The miller spoke to her, "I have gained great wealth through you. I shall take care of you in splendor as long as you live."

But she answered, "I cannot remain here. I will go away. Compassionate people will give me as much as I need."

Then she had her mutilated arms tied to her back, and at sunrise she set forth, walking the entire day until it was night. She came to a royal garden, and by the light of the moon, she saw that inside there were trees full of beautiful fruit. But she could not get inside, for it was surrounded by water.

Having walked the entire day without eating a bite, she was suffering from hunger, and she thought, "Oh, if only I were inside the garden so I could eat of those fruits. Otherwise, I shall perish."

Then she kneeled down and, crying out to God the Lord, she prayed. Suddenly an angel appeared. He closed a head gate so that the moat dried up, and she could walk through.

She entered the garden, and the angel went with her. She saw a fruit tree with beautiful pears, but they had all been counted. She stepped up to the tree and ate from it with her mouth, enough to satisfy her hunger, but no more. The gardener saw it happen, but because the angel was standing by her he was afraid and thought that the girl was a spirit. He said nothing and did not dare to call out nor to speak to the spirit. After she had eaten the pear, she was full and she went and lay down in the brush.

The king who owned this garden came the next morning. He counted the fruit and saw that one of the pears was missing. He asked the gardener what had happened to it. It was not lying under the tree but had somehow disappeared.

The gardener answered, "Last night a spirit came here. It had no hands and ate one of the pears with its mouth."

The king said, "How did the spirit get across the water? And where did it go after it had eaten the pear?"

The gardener answered, "Someone dressed in snow-white came from heaven and closed the head gate so the spirit could walk through the moat. Because it must have been an angel I was afraid, and I asked no questions, and I did not call out. After the spirit had eaten the pear it went away again."

The king said, "If what you said is true, I will keep watch with you tonight."

After it was dark the king entered the garden, bringing a priest with him who was to talk to the spirit. All three sat down under the tree and kept watch. At midnight the girl came creeping out of the brush, stepped up to the tree, and again ate off a pear with her mouth. An angel dressed in white was standing next to her.

The priest walked up to them and said, "Have you come from God, or from the world? Are you a spirit or a human?"

She answered, "I am not a spirit, but a poor human who has been abandoned by everyone except God."

The king said, "Even if you have been abandoned by the whole world, I will not abandon you."

He took her home with him to his royal castle, and because she was so beautiful and pure, he loved her with all his heart, had silver hands made for her, and took her as his wife.

After a year the king had to go out into the battlefield, and he left the young queen in the care of his mother, saying, "If she has a child, support her and take good care of her, and immediately send me the news in a letter."

She gave birth to a beautiful son. The old mother quickly wrote this in a letter, giving the joyful news to the king.

Now on the way, the messenger stopped at a brook to rest. Tired from his long journey, he fell asleep. Then the devil came to him. He still wanted to harm the pious queen, and he took the letter, putting in its place one that stated that the queen had brought a changeling into the world. When the king read this letter he was frightened and saddened, but nevertheless, he wrote an answer that they should take good care of the queen until his return. The messenger returned with this letter, but he rested at the same place, and again fell asleep. The devil came again and placed a different letter in his bag. This letter said that they should kill the queen with her child.

The old mother was terribly frightened when she received this letter. She could not believe it and wrote to the king again, but she got back the same answer because each time the devil substituted a false letter. And the last letter even stated that they should keep the queen's tongue and eyes as proof.

The old mother lamented that such innocent blood was to be shed, and in the night she had a doe killed, cut out its tongue and eyes, and had them put aside.

Then she said to the queen, "I cannot have you killed as the king has ordered, but you can no longer stay here. Go out into the wide world with your child, and never come back."

The old mother tied the queen's child onto her back, and the poor woman went away with weeping eyes. She came to a great, wild

121

forest where she got onto her knees and prayed to God. Then the angel of the Lord appeared to her and led her to a small house. On it was a small sign with the words, "Here anyone can live free."

A snow-white virgin came from the house and said, "Welcome, Queen," and then led her inside. She untied the small boy from her back, held him to her breast so he could drink, and then laid him in a beautiful made-up bed.

Then the poor woman said, "How did you know that I am a queen?"

The white virgin answered, "I am an angel, sent by God to take care of you and your child."

She stayed in this house for seven years and was well taken care of. And through the grace of God and her own piety, her chopped-off hands grew back.

The king finally came back home from the battlefield, and the first thing he wanted to do was to see his wife and their child.

Then the old mother began to weep, saying, "You wicked man, why did you write to me that I was to put two innocent souls to death?" and she showed him the two letters that the evil one had counterfeited. Then she continued to speak, "I did what you ordered," and showed him as proof the eyes and the tongue.

Then the king began to weep even more bitterly for his poor wife and his little son, until the old woman had mercy and said to him, "Be satisfied that she is still alive. I secretly had a doe killed and took the proofs from it. I tied your wife's child onto her back and told her to go out into the wide world, and she had to promise never to come back here because you were so angry with her."

Then the king said, "I will go as far as the sky is blue, and will neither eat nor drink until I have found my dear wife and my child again, provided that in the meantime they have not died or perished from hunger."

Then the king traveled about for nearly seven years, searching in all the stone cliffs and caves, but he did not find her, and he thought that she had perished. He neither ate nor drank during the entire time, but God kept him alive. Finally, he came to a great forest, where he found a little house with a sign containing the words, " Here anyone can live free."

The white virgin came out, took him by the hand, led him inside, and said, "Welcome, King," then asked him where he had come from.

He answered, "I have been traveling about for nearly seven years looking for my wife and her child, but I cannot find them."

The angel offered him something to eat and drink, but he did not take it, wanting only to rest a little. He lay down to sleep, covering his face with a cloth.

Then the angel went into the room where the queen was sitting with her son, whom she normally called "Filled-with-Grief."

The angel said to her, "Go into the next room with your child. Your husband has come."

She went to where he was lying, and the cloth fell from his face.

Then she said, "Filled-with-Grief, pick up the cloth for your father and put it over his face again."

The child picked it up and put it over his face again. The king heard this in his sleep and let the cloth fall again.

Then the little boy grew impatient and said, "Mother, dear, how can I cover my father's face? I have no father in this world. I have learned to pray, 'Our father which art in heaven,' and you have said that my father is in heaven and that he is our dear God. How can I know such a wild man? He is not my father."

Hearing this, the king arose and asked who she was.

She said, "I am your wife, and this is your son Filled-with-Grief."

He saw her living hands and said, "My wife had silver hands."

She answered, "Our merciful God has caused my natural hands to grow back."

The angel went into the other room, brought back the silver hands, and showed them to him. Now he saw for sure that it was his dear wife and his dear child, and he kissed them, and rejoiced, and said, "A heavy stone has fallen from my heart."

Then the angel of God gave them all something to eat, and they went back home to his old mother. There was great joy everywhere, and the king and the queen conducted their wedding ceremony once again, and they lived happily until their blessed end.

The Robotic Finger

Once upon a time, there was a brilliant and highly skilled vascular surgeon. He was well respected in the hospital and the community, especially when he turned on his charm, as time or circumstance required. Many thought he had a perfect life, considering the number of people he had helped over the years, but he did not. His life at home and work was far from perfect.

Though his surgical skills were admired, his arrogant demeanor at work and his immense ego isolated him from his peers and left only a handful of people willing to work with him. He would brag that they were hand-picked by him. To some degree, they were, because they had "lasted," and were no longer berated for incompetence. Rarely did they ever hear a compliment uttered after a complicated procedure or a very long day of work, but they enjoyed seeing the many positive outcomes so they endured the less than collegial work environment.

Psychologists would have referred to the individuals who worked with him as encountering "battered wife syndrome." They had all managed to withstand the verbal abuse and dodged the medical instruments that flew through the air in the early years and were now no longer worried when in the operating room with him. He called them the "A-Team" for one reason but the staff members called themselves the "A-Team" for another, omitting the word "hole" except when they were alone or out for drinks, and they had come to wear that badge with pride. He was still verbally abusive, but they were able to ignore that because they understood it was directed mostly at himself and not them, due to his need to be a perfectionist in everything he did.

He was meticulous about every aspect of the operating room processes and the staff would often comment that he "performed miracles." They had heard him make that exact claim on numerous occasions and then attribute it to his "special hands." They just shrugged their shoulders now when they heard it, or rolled their eyes when he wasn't looking. His ego required that miracle worker label and they accepted it because he was indeed immensely talented. His scrub nurse was not only impressed with his skill, but also his fastidious attention to infection control. She could think of only one surgical site infection occurring in the many years she had worked with him and that was a remarkable achievement.

His wife was demanding in every aspect of his life at home. On his days away from work, she consumed every moment of his attention. He found this sweet and endearing at first, but it quickly became parasitic. She liked to host lavish parties and often stayed up late, sometimes until the sun came up. It became obvious that she was using illegal drugs to fuel her activities. He warned her several times to stop but she ignored him. She was often able to persuade him to join her, especially when she got him behind closed doors and bathed his ego with drug-induced sexual pleasures that she offered and provided.

He realized this drug habit was harmful and decided he had to stop, and so he did. He had excellent control of his mind and body. Years of delicate surgical training and experience had instilled discipline and his ego in this sense was an asset, not a liability. His actions were robotic when he wanted to behave in a particular way, and he could become impervious to temptation and solely concentrate on work if he chose to do so. One day, he gave his wife an ultimatum; if she didn't stop using drugs, he would divorce her. She didn't believe him, but even her prolific sexual attributes and beauty could not sway him from his threat. One year to the day after he ordered her to stop, he divorced her.

She demanded a lot of money from him and threatened to blackmail him if necessary. He wasn't worried and suggested she go ahead and try that. He knew what would happen. Both would have to submit to drug tests and he would pass them and she would fail. With those results, the judge would throw out her argument as spurious and possibly hold her for contempt and extortion. He would ask the judge to be lenient, which would show everyone how kind he was, especially when he gave her $50,000, the sports car that was in his name, and let her keep her expensive jewelry. All he wanted from the divorce was to keep his house and to get his life back, and he knew he would achieve both of those goals.

When the divorce was final, it was as if the marriage had just been an interruption in his life. He got a lot of "sorrys" right after the divorce, and he graciously accepted them and would always add that he hoped his ex-wife got her life in order. Those who didn't know him well would nod and think what a good man he was. Those who truly knew him understood it was just a way for him to assuage his ego, and build upon the "charming and grateful" persona he wanted to project. But within several weeks the drama had subsided and everything was back to normal. His life's focus became that at which he was most adept: changing people's lives by performing non-routine lifesaving surgeries which he was able to make look routine each time he did them.

He was a very athletic man who loved to ski and he planned a ski trip for himself, his scrub nurse, scrub tech, and primary radiology technologist over the Thanksgiving break. He had worked them hard during the year, especially after the divorce, and he wanted to make a grand gesture to show his appreciation. So, he bought plane tickets for them and their significant others and covered the expenses for their hotel rooms, meals, and drinks. It was a tremendous gift and certainly accomplished what he hoped for. It endeared him to them and made them want to work even harder for him. The "thank yous" lasted well into the following year and each time he heard another doctor or staff member whispering about what he had done, his ego grew a little bit more.

They all had a wonderful time on the trip, but he suffered an accident on the last day and injured his spine. What was most concerning to him was the injury to the T1 vertebrae, which he knew would affect the nerves in his forearm and his ability to move his fingers.

He could have tried anti-inflammatory drugs and physical therapy to fix the problem, but he was too impatient to wait and see if they would help. Instead, he elected to have decompression surgery. It was successful but he was in a lot of pain afterward and a surgical friend prescribed Oxycontin for him, knowing that he would never allow himself to develop a dependency. And just as everyone assumed, two weeks after surgery and rehab therapy, he had flipped the switch on his robotic mind and was back to performing surgery.

He told himself he would only take the Oxycontin for a month and after that, he would be fine without it. He told himself that, but that is not what occurred. He convinced himself the drug provided the stamina necessary to stand for hours during a difficult surgical procedure. His mind had successfully overcome addictive elements of his life in the past but failed him this time because he allowed his ego to intervene and control the process.

He ignored the first signs and symptoms of dependency but in due time the seductive pain relief and the euphoria effect from the drug took hold of his body. However, his precision in the operating room was still present, so he knew that those who worked with him would not notice he was developing an addiction, even though each day he was becoming more of a danger to himself and those around him.

It was after a long day of surgery, one in which he needed several pills to get through the lengthy operation, that he stopped off at the bar on his way home and had several drinks. He convinced himself he was fine when he got in the car and started driving home. He did not notice the three people crossing the road on the dark neighborhood street. He hit all three of them while traveling at a high speed.

He did not stop until he got home. The front end of his truck had only minor body damage but he could tell by the extent of the brain and bone fragments, blood, and spinal fluid that was present, that the injured probably did not survive. He went inside and swallowed another pill with a large glass of vodka, hoping he would pass out, but his brain allowed him no peace.

He retraced the drive home in his mind. At first, he only saw three shadows but then the faces of the man and the woman came into focus; eyes wide open and in shock at what was about to happen. He could never see the third face but he didn't want to see it. He knew he would be haunted by what he had done for a very long time. He closed his eyes and tried to think of what he should do if he received a call from the hospital. That call came about an hour after the accident.

He was told there was a traumatic injury to a young woman who needed his expertise. He listened while her injuries were described to him and after he had gathered all of the medical information that he needed, he told them to stabilize her, start administering antibiotics, and prep her for surgery. He got up, showered, drank three cups of black coffee, and headed to the hospital in his car.

As soon as he walked into the operating room, he felt fine physically and was ready to atone for the crime he had committed earlier. When he looked at the injured young woman he had to step back for a moment and catch his breath. He realized the woman standing next to him wasn't his regular scrub nurse. His scrub nurse was lying on the table with a fractured pelvis, legs that looked like they had been blown apart by a bomb, and chest and arm injuries that suggested she had been hit by construction equipment. His brain was screaming "NO!" but he knew he needed to do everything he could to save his friend and in doing so, hopefully, salvage some part of his soul.

He worked for eight straight hours with the orthopedic surgeon as they tried to save her legs but were unsuccessful. They had to amputate both of them just above the knee and hope for the best. He was optimistic that he had saved her arms and hands even though the microsurgery needed for her hands was more extensive than he had ever performed on one person. He spent several hours in the ICU with her to make sure she was stable before he went home to try to sleep.

He turned on his television at home and heard the news about the terrible accident that had killed a father and mother and sent their daughter to the hospital. As soon as the reporter said the police had no leads, he turned off the tv. He lay in bed and remembered how his wife had tried to take everything he had from him. He wondered what he would do if someone killed his mother and father and caused him to lose his legs. He knew the answer without even hesitating. He would want to kill them.

The next day, he went by the ICU to check on his friend's hands. He berated the nurses, telling them they weren't getting enough circulation and as a result, he would now need to do additional surgery. The surgery went well, but her hands became infected with necrotizing fasciitis. He had to amputate them to save her life. He spent most of the next week by her side and when she woke up, he was there to explain what had happened. When she asked about her parents, he quietly told her they were dead. She was much more upset at losing them than the fact she no longer had legs or hands. He prescribed strong sedatives for her and told her she just needed to rest. She said she would try to rest now, but when she got well, she would find the person who did this to her and her parents. He simply said he understood as he watched the sedative take over her ability to talk and she fell into a deep sleep.

He went home and washed his truck as if he was scouring an operating room, and then went inside and sat down. He took a pain pill and began to rationalize. There was nothing else he could do. There was nothing. They were dead and she was alive, thanks to him, and he needed to be around to help other people. His longtime faithful nurse would surely understand that. His abilities were needed. He would stop the pills today and dedicate the rest of his life to helping people through his surgical talent. And just as in the past, he switched into the mechanical mode and stopped taking the pills that very night.

He visited his friend often and she got better with each passing day, learning how to live in her new world. She told him that if everything continued to heal on schedule, she would be fitted for prosthetic limbs for her legs in about six weeks. He smiled and said if there was anything she needed he would be there to help her.

Six weeks later, at a memorial service for her parents, he saw her walking on her new limbs with the use of crutches. After the service, he expressed his pride in her ability to move forward. She told him that she was just as driven as he was and he smiled, acknowledging her comment as true. She told him that she was going to Europe for a few months but hoped to see him when she came back. He said that he looked forward to it.

Over the next six months, he maintained his sobriety regarding opiates and continued to make good on his promise to help others. Driving home, he hesitated every so often at the place he had hit his nurse and her parents but then put the guilt behind him. One evening, after getting home and opening his liquor cabinet, he found two Oxycontin pills pushed back in the corner of it.

He stared at them for a few minutes and told himself he could take those two and be fine. It was just two little pills and he deserved them, considering everything he had been through. So, he swallowed them and then drank several large glasses of vodka before he fell asleep on the sofa. When he awoke, he was lying in his bed on top of bloody sheets. He screamed when he saw what was on the bedside table.

He heard the voice before he saw the person sitting in the shadows. He didn't have to see the face to know who it was.

"I never saw my hands after I lost them, so I can imagine seeing yours laying there on the table must be very traumatic. Especially because, knowing you and your ego, you will be thinking your hands were more special than anyone else's. But they were just hands, able to perform exquisite surgery from years and years of training. That same ego you have that makes you a great surgeon, also makes you think you're superhuman. But you're not. In fact, right now I would say you were less than human.

"After all, you did commit murder. You killed my parents and left me for dead. At a minimum, that would be considered vehicular homicide.

But then when you realized what you had done, you allowed my hands to get infected. I know you. That didn't happen unless you planned for it to happen. You do not tolerate infections. That was one of the things that I once admired about you. The way you made sure your patients had the best chance to recover, without any life-altering infections. I knew the low rate of infection that you maintained was just your way of showing the other doctors how much better you were than them, but I didn't care. It was best for the patients.

"So, when I got an infection, I knew what had happened. You were trying to prevent me from coming back and killing you. You can try and deny it, but it won't work with me. You underestimated my willpower and my ability. Just look at these hands. Aren't they something? I got them in Sweden. I can't do microsurgery with them but I can do most other things.

"Electrodes were implanted in my muscles and nerves and this system they created sends signals in both directions, from prosthesis to brain and back. Heck, I can even administer anesthetic and operate this little hand saw that I used to cut off your hands. By the way, I wasn't very concerned with being sterile. I just put on the tourniquet and sawed right through the bones. Then I cauterized the wounds so you wouldn't bleed to death. I can only imagine, once the sedation wears off, how those nubs are going to hurt like a son of a bitch.

"I saw you that night, you know. I'm surprised you didn't see my face. Maybe you did but told yourself you didn't. I could see how your mind could allow that to occur. But I should have seen this coming. I thought you were becoming addicted to those pain pills and I should have spoken up but I didn't. That is something that we both have to live with now.

"I left a couple of pills for you in the liquor cabinet, because I know you. You just figured they were there from your past and your ego told yourself, 'I can have those two, and I will be fine.' How predictable.

"Didn't you know we all worked with you because we knew you would give the patient the best outcome? We overlooked the fact you were an asshole because we could see that if we gave you what you needed and let your wonderful trained mind make those 'magical hands' work, patient's lives were improved and at times saved. But you don't see it. It's your mind, not your hands, that make you what you are.

"The rest of the bottle of pain pills is over there on the dresser for when the numbness wears off. I don't know how you're going to open them without your magic hands, but I'm sure you'll figure it out. I just hope you don't get addicted again. But that robotic mind of yours won't allow that to happen, will it? You can just compartmentalize everything and move forward as if nothing happened. Right?

"Unfortunately, I couldn't. I loved my parents dearly and they didn't deserve to die the way they did. Left there on the side of the road, like roadkill. They were alive for a while after you hit them. If you had only stopped, I bet you could have saved them. Even in your state, you could have done something to save them. But, you didn't. You didn't stop."

"No, I didn't stop. I should have. I am so sorry. Forgive me. Oh God, please forgive me."

"Damn. I should think of becoming a psychic because I knew you'd say that. That damn ego of yours. It thinks I can forgive you for what you did, but I can't forgive you. I am recording this conversation, by the way. Even have the video of my surgery. All you have to do is admit what you did to the police: how you hit three people and left them to die, and how you took my hands off on purpose. Once you do that, I will gladly admit I removed your hands and show them the video. But the psychic part of me is telling me your ego won't let you do that. But I'll be around, just in case.

"Oh, and just one more thing," she said as she raised her robotic middle finger. "You need to get some of these hands," she added as she turned and walked out of the room.

The Death of the Little Hen

Once upon a time the little hen and the little rooster went to Nut Mountain, and they agreed that whoever would find a nut would share it with the other one. Now the little hen found a large, large nut, but -- wanting to eat the kernel by herself -- she said nothing about it. However, the kernel was so thick that she could not swallow it down. It got stuck in her throat, and fearing that she would choke to death, she cried out, "Little Rooster, I beg you to run as fast as you can to the well and get me some water, or else I'll choke to death."

The little rooster ran to the well as fast as he could, and said, "Well, give me some water, for the little hen is lying on Nut Mountain. She swallowed a large nut kernel and is about to choke to death on it."

The well answered, "First run to the bride, and get some red silk from her."

The little rooster ran to the bride: "Bride, give me some red silk, and I'll give the red silk to the well, and the well will give me some water, and I'll take the water to the little hen who is lying on Nut Mountain. She swallowed a large nut kernel and is about to choke to death on it."

The bride answered, "First run and get my wreath. It got caught on a willow branch."

So the little rooster ran to the willow and pulled the wreath from its branch and took it to the bride, and the bride gave him some red silk, which he took to the well, which gave him some water, and the little rooster took the water to the little hen, but when he arrived, she had already choked to death, and she lay there dead and did not move at all.

The little rooster was so sad that he cried aloud, and all the animals came to mourn for the little hen. Six mice built a small carriage which was to carry the little hen to her grave. When the carriage was finished, they hitched themselves to it, and the little rooster drove. On the way, they met the fox.

"Where are you going, little rooster?"

"I'm going to bury my little hen."

"May I ride along?"

"Yes, but you must sit at the rear because my little horses don't like you too close to the front."

So he sat at the rear, and then the wolf, the bear, the elk, the lion, and all the animals in the forest. They rode on until they came to a brook. "How can we get across?" asked the little rooster.

A straw was lying there next to the brook, and he said, "I'll lay myself across, and you can drive over me." But just as the six mice got onto the straw, it slipped into the water, and the six mice all fell in and drowned.

They did not know what to do, until a coal came and said, "I am large enough. I will lay myself across and you can drive over me." So the coal laid itself across the water, but unfortunately, it touched the water, hissed, and went out; and it was dead.

A stone saw this happen and wanting to help the little rooster, it laid itself across the water. The little rooster pulled the carriage himself. He nearly reached the other side with the dead little hen, but there were too many others seated on the back of the carriage, and the carriage rolled back, and they all fell into the water and drowned.

Now the little rooster was all alone with the dead little hen. He dug a grave for her and laid her inside. Then he made a mound on top, and sat on it, and grieved there so long that he too died. And then every one was dead.

Criminal

Once upon a time, two gangs fought each other almost daily for control of the areas in which they lived. One gang thought they should control a block that was dominated by their rivals. Their rivals thought they should control two blocks of their adversary's territory, and so their lust for power created many "accidents" for the police to investigate.

As long as the gangs only killed each other, the police were not interested in spending too much time investigating their deaths. The police captain in charge of gang activities told his staff, "If it's a gang member, just pick up the body and notify the parents or next of kin, provided you can find them." The police chief's indifference was not criticized by any of the citizens living in those areas. They understood. In fact, when they learned that a gang member had died, they often held private parties to celebrate so that the gangs did not know they were applauding their oppressor's death. Ironically, the gang's apathy for the sanctity of life and subsequent death had become a reason to celebrate life.

Even the names of the gangs reflected their blatant disregard for justice and societal norms. The tattoos that they had burned into their skin identified them as a member of "The Murderers" or "The Killers." The symbols of death spray-painted onto buildings marked their territory like animals and warned everyone of whose concrete wilderness they were traversing. The graffiti was meant to intimidate and cause fear in anyone who saw it and it worked. The public displays of burned or headless bodies helped reinforce that anxiety and dread.

The churches and religious leaders had moved their buildings and services out of those neighborhoods because they could not risk anyone else being killed by an errant bullet, which had happened on more than one occasion. They only made "missionary trips" into those areas and though they tried to change the gang's perspective on life and death, they could not make any of them see that the only outcome that awaited them was a bloody and deadly one.

Most shopkeepers and stores had also left the vicinity, but those who stayed boarded up their windows with plywood and put metal bars on the doors. Some even had metal doors they could pull down in front of their store and lock after they closed, but those restraints were more psychological feelings of security for the owner than deterrents for either gang. The only stores that were not looted or burned to the ground were those whose owners paid one of the gangs for protection. Even then, they were still afraid of their protectors and lived in fear that one day the opposing gang would come for them, either as a way to get money for their own protection or as a way to show the other gang their means of protection were inadequate.

Family members of the gangs had moved away or were in the process of doing so. They understood what their sons or daughters had become and knew the costly initiation fee to join the club. They could not risk a brother or sister or any other family member dying to elicit fear or exact revenge. It had happened before and they had come to the realization that they could not change the way of life for their misguided son or daughter. "Better to lose one son or daughter than two," they told themselves. They mourned the loss of their 'gang member' child as if they were already dead because they knew their spiritual being had died and was only awaiting the physical vessel to join it. They knew it, but they still prayed for the lost child's soul and for their own forgiveness, and they, almost daily, wept for change.

One hot summer, there were thirteen killings in one weekend. The following week, while several funerals were taking place, even more murders occurred as the rival gangs sought revenge. Bullet holes entered the caskets as if the shooter thought they could kill a dead person again. It was their way of demonstrating hatred for the slain and striking fear within the living.

The police investigated those murders with a strong intent to find the culprits but they could not identify the person or persons who committed the crimes. They had disappeared into the vacant buildings as if they were ghosts. Some of the living even suggested to the police they were indeed "ghosts" or "demons" that traversed from one world to the other. Though the police didn't believe that, they could not find them and eventually it became just another cold case with very little evidence.

After the many funerals, both of the gang leaders agreed to a meeting to try and resolve the territorial disputes. They were losing members faster than they could replenish their armies now that most of the families had moved away, and both groups wanted to quell the slaughter. At least until one of them knew they had the upper hand.

The meeting was set up in an abandoned building in the middle of the war zone and the gang leaders agreed to certain rules of engagement. They could only be accompanied by one bodyguard and their second in command. They would all come armed, basing that decision on the fact that if everyone knew they were armed, there would be less chance of a shooting at the meeting. Five gang members from each group were required to go to the other gang's headquarters and wait for the end of the meeting. If someone other than those assigned to the meeting were spotted within a block of the building, then one of those gang members would be killed for every person that had ventured into the established meeting perimeter. This, they reasoned, would be a way to keep everyone else away and reduce the likelihood of a lapse in judgment whereupon a stray bullet might go through someone's head.

The day came and the meeting took place. The gang leaders sat across from each other at a folding table with their bodyguard and second in command on either side of them. The first thing that they agreed to do was have everyone hold their guns. The gang leaders both nodded their heads as if they had accomplished something significant. Territories were discussed and another agreement was reached in which "The Murderers" would give up the block that "The Killers" wanted, provided that the gang leader of the "The Murderers" would be allowed to kill "The Killers" second in command.

"The Killers" second in command looked at "The Murderers" gang leader and immediately shot his second in command. As soon as he did that, "The Murderers" gang leader shot "The Killers" second in command, whereupon "The Killers" gang leader shot "The Murderers" gang leader. "The Murderers" bodyguard then shot "The Killers" gang leader, at which point "The Killers" bodyguard shot "The Murderers" bodyguard, leaving him as the sole survivor.

Since some of the victims were still breathing, "The Killers" bodyguard walked around to each one and put a bullet in their head. He smiled as he understood he would now be the leader of both gangs because he had survived what would become a legendary moment among all the gang members. He carved out the tattoos of each person that would identify them to their respective gangs and then placed them in his back pockets. He felt the blood drip down his pants and he enjoyed the feeling as he walked out of the building. When he stepped into the alley, several of the pieces of skin fell out onto the ground and as he bent over to retrieve them, a car swerved into his head, almost decapitating him. The drunk driver drove away quickly realizing he had killed a gang member. He was never found.

Brother Lustig

O nce upon a time, there was a great war, and when it came to an end, many soldiers were discharged. Then Brother Lustig also received his dismissal, and besides that, nothing but a small loaf of contract-bread, and four kreuzers in money, with which he departed. St. Peter had, however, placed himself in his way in the shape of a poor beggar, and when Brother Lustig came up, he begged alms of him. Brother Lustig replied, "Dear beggar-man, what am I to give you? I have been a soldier, and have received my dismissal, and have nothing but this little loaf of contract-bread, and four kreuzers of money; when that is gone, I shall have to beg as well as you. Still, I will give you something."

Thereupon he divided the loaf into four parts and gave the apostle one of them, and a kreuzer likewise. St. Peter thanked him, went onwards, and threw himself again in the soldier's way as a beggar, but in another shape; and when he came up begged a gift of him as before. Brother Lustig spoke as he had done before, and again gave him a quarter of the loaf and one kreuzer. St. Peter thanked him, and went onwards, but for the third time placed himself in another shape as a beggar on the road, and spoke to Brother Lustig. Brother Lustig gave him also the third quarter of bread and the third kreuzer. St. Peter thanked him, and Brother Lustig went onwards and had but a quarter of the loaf and one kreuzer. With that, he went into an inn, ate the bread, and ordered one kreuzer's worth of beer. When he had had it, he journeyed onwards.

Then St. Peter, who had assumed the appearance of a discharged soldier, met and spoke to him thus: "Good day, comrade, canst thou not give me a bit of bread, and a kreuzer to get a drink?"

"Where am I to procure it?" answered Brother Lustig; "I have been discharged, and I got nothing but a loaf of ammunition-bread and four kreuzers in money. I met three beggars on the road, and I gave each of them a quarter of my bread and one kreuzer. The last quarter I ate in the inn and had a drink with the last kreuzer. Now my pockets are empty, and if thou also hast nothing we can go a-begging together."

"No," answered St. Peter, "we need not quite do that. I know a little about medicine, and I will soon earn as much as I require by that."

"Indeed," said Brother Lustig, "I know nothing of that, so I must go and beg alone."

"Just come with me," said St. Peter, "and if I earn anything, thou shalt have half of it."

"All right," said Brother Lustig, so they went away together. Then they came to a peasant's house inside which they heard loud lamentations and cries; so they went in, and there the husband was lying sick unto death, and very near his end, and his wife was crying and weeping quite loudly. "Stop that howling and crying," said St. Peter, "I will make the man well again," and he took a salve out of his pocket, and healed the sick man in a moment, so that he could get up, and was in perfect health. In great delight, the man and his wife said, "How can we reward you? What shall we give you?"

But St. Peter would take nothing, and the more the peasant folks offered him, the more he refused. Brother Lustig, however, nudged St. Peter, and said, "Take something; sure enough we are in need of it." At length, the woman brought a lamb and said to St. Peter that he really must take that, but he would not. Then Brother Lustig gave him a poke in the side, and said, "Do take it, you stupid fool; we are in great want of it!" Then St. Peter said at last, "Well, I will take the lamb, but I won't carry it; if thou wilt insist on having it, thou must carry it."

"That is nothing," said Brother Lustig, "I will easily carry it," and took it on his shoulder. Then they departed and came to a wood, but Brother Lustig had begun to feel the lamb heavy, and he was hungry, so he said to St. Peter, "Look, that's a good place, we might cook the lamb there, and eat it."

"As you like," answered St. Peter, "but I can't have anything to do with the cooking; if thou wilt cook, there is a kettle for thee, and in the meantime, I will walk about a little until it is ready. Thou must, however, not begin to eat until I have come back, I will come at the right time."

"Well, go, then," said Brother Lustig, "I understand cookery, I will manage it." Then St. Peter went away, and Brother Lustig killed the lamb, lighted a fire, threw the meat into the kettle, and boiled it. The lamb was, however, quite ready, and the apostle Peter had not come back, so Brother Lustig took it out of the kettle, cut it up, and found the heart. "That is said to be the best part," said he, and tasted it, but at last he ate it all up.

At length, St. Peter returned and said, "Thou mayst eat the whole of the lamb thyself, I will only have the heart, give me that." Then Brother Lustig took a knife and fork and pretended to look anxiously about amongst the lamb's flesh, but not to be able to find the heart, and at last, he said abruptly, "There is none here."

"But where can it be?" said the apostle.

142

"I don't know," replied Brother Lustig, "but look, what fools we both are, to seek for the lamb's heart, and neither of us to remember that a lamb has no heart!"

"Oh," said St. Peter, "that is something quite new! Every animal has a heart, why is a lamb to have none?"

"No, be assured, my brother," said Brother Lustig, "that a lamb has no heart; just consider it seriously, and then you will see that it really has none."

"Well, it is all right," said St. Peter, "if there is no heart, then I want none of the lamb; thou mayst eat it alone."

"What I can't eat now, I will carry away in my knapsack," said Brother Lustig, and he ate half the lamb, and put the rest in his knapsack.

They went farther, and then St. Peter caused a great stream of water to flow right across their path, and they were obliged to pass through it. Said St. Peter, "Do thou go first."

"No," answered Brother Lustig, "thou must go first," and he thought, "if the water is too deep I will stay behind." Then St. Peter strode through it, and the water just reached to his knee. So, Brother Lustig began to go through also, but the water grew deeper and reached to his throat. Then he cried, "Brother, help me!"

St. Peter said, "Then wilt thou confess that thou hast eaten the lamb's heart?"

"No," said he, "I have not eaten it." Then the water grew deeper still and rose to his mouth. "Help me, brother!" cried the soldier.

St. Peter said, "Then wilt thou confess that thou hast eaten the lamb's heart?"

143

"No," he replied, "I have not eaten it." St. Peter, however, would not let him be drowned, but made the water sink and helped him through it.

Then they journeyed onwards and came to a kingdom where they heard that the King's daughter lay sick unto death. "Hello, brother!" said the soldier to St. Peter, "this is a chance for us; if we can heal her we shall be provided for, for life!" But St. Peter was not half quick enough for him, "Come, lift your legs, my dear brother," said he, "that we may get there in time." But St. Peter walked slower and slower, though Brother Lustig did all he could to drive and push him on, and at last they heard that the princess was dead. "Now we are done for!" said Brother Lustig; "that comes of thy sleepy way of walking!"

"Just be quiet," answered St. Peter, "I can do more than cure sick people; I can bring dead ones to life again."

"Well, if thou canst do that," said Brother Lustig, "it's all right, but thou shouldst earn at least half the kingdom for us by that."

Then they went to the royal palace, where everyone was in great grief, but St. Peter told the King that he would restore his daughter to life. He was taken to her, and said, "Bring me a kettle and some water," and when that was brought, he bade everyone go out, and allowed no one to remain with him but Brother Lustig. Then he cut off all the dead girl's limbs, and threw them in the water, lighted a fire beneath the kettle, and boiled them. And when the flesh had fallen away from the bones, he took out the beautiful white bones, and laid them on a table, and arranged them together in their natural order.

When he had done that, he stepped forward and said three times, "In the name of the holy Trinity, dead woman, arise." And at the third time, the princess arose, living, healthy and beautiful. Then the King was in the greatest joy, and said to St. Peter, "Ask for thy reward; even if it were half my kingdom, I would give it thee." But St. Peter said, "I want nothing for it."

"Oh, thou tomfool!" thought Brother Lustig to himself, and nudged his comrade's side, and said, "Don't be so stupid! If thou hast no need of anything, I have." St. Peter, however, would have nothing, but as the King saw that the other would very much like to have something, he ordered his treasurer to fill Brother Lustig's knapsack with gold.

Then they went on their way, and when they came to a forest, St. Peter said to Brother Lustig, "Now, we will divide the gold."

"Yes," he replied, "we will." So, St. Peter divided the gold and divided it into three heaps. Brother Lustig thought to himself, "What craze has he got in his head now? He is making three shares, and there are only two of us!" But St. Peter said, "I have divided it exactly; there is one share for me, one for thee, and one for him who ate the lamb's heart."

"Oh, I ate that!" replied Brother Lustig, and hastily swept up the gold. "You may trust what I say."

"But how can that be true," asked St. Peter, "when a lamb has no heart?"

"Eh, what, brother, what can you be thinking of? Lambs have hearts like other animals, why should they only have none?"

"Well, so be it," said St. Peter, "keep the gold to yourself, but I will stay with you no longer; I will go my way alone."

"As you like, dear brother," answered Brother Lustig. "Farewell."

Then St. Peter went a different road, but Brother Lustig thought, "It is a good thing that he has taken himself off, he is a strange saint, after all." Then he had money enough, but did not know how to manage it, squandered it, gave it away, and when some time had gone by, once more had nothing. Then he arrived in a certain country where he heard that the King's daughter was dead. "Oh, ho!" thought he, "that may be a good thing for me; I will bring her to life again, and see that I am paid as I ought to be." So, he went to the King and offered to raise the dead girl to life again.

Now the King had heard that a discharged soldier was traveling about and bringing dead persons to life again, and thought that Brother Lustig was the man; but as he had no confidence in him, he consulted his councilors first, who said that he might give it a trial as his daughter was dead. Then Brother Lustig ordered water to be brought to him in a kettle, bade everyone go out, cut the limbs off, threw them in the water, and lighted a fire beneath, just as he had seen St. Peter do. The water began to boil, the flesh fell off, and then he took the bones out and laid them on the table, but he did not know the order in which to lay them, and placed them all wrong and in confusion. Then he stood before them and said, "In the name of the most holy Trinity, dead maiden, I bid thee arise," and he said this thrice, but the bones did not stir. So, he said it thrice more, but also in vain: "Confounded girl that you are, get up!" cried he, "Get up, or it shall be worse for you!"

When he had said that St. Peter suddenly appeared in his former shape as a discharged soldier; he entered by the window and said, "Godless man, what art thou doing? How can the dead maiden arise, when thou hast thrown about her bones in such confusion?"

"Dear brother, I have done everything to the best of my ability," he answered.

"This once, I will help thee out of thy difficulty, but one thing I tell thee, and that is that if ever thou undertakest anything of the

146

kind again, it will be the worse for thee, and also that thou must neither demand nor accept the smallest thing from the King for this!" Thereupon, St. Peter laid the bones in their right order, said to the maiden three times, "In the name of the most holy Trinity, dead maiden, arise," and the King's daughter arose, healthy and beautiful as before.

Then St. Peter went away again by the window, and Brother Lustig was rejoiced to find that all had passed off so well, but was very much vexed to think that after all, he was not to take anything for it. "I should just like to know," thought he, "what fancy that fellow has got in his head, for what he gives with one hand he takes away with the other -- there is no sense whatever in it!" Then the King offered Brother Lustig whatsoever he wished to have, but he did not dare to take anything; however, by hints and cunning, he contrived to make the King order his knapsack to be filled with gold for him, and with that, he departed.

When he got out, St. Peter was standing by the door, and said, "Just look what a man thou art; did I not forbid thee to take anything, and there thou hast thy knapsack full of gold!"

"How can I help that," answered Brother Lustig, "if people will put it in for me?"

"Well, I tell thee this, that if ever thou settest about anything of this kind again thou shalt suffer for it!"

"Eh, brother, have no fear now I have money, why should I trouble myself with washing bones?"

"Faith," said St. Peter, "the gold will last a long time! In order that after this thou mayst never tread in forbidden paths, I will bestow on thy knapsack this property, namely, that whatsoever thou wishest to have inside it, shall be there. Farewell, thou wilt now never see me more."

"Goodbye," said Brother Lustig, and thought to himself, "I am very glad that thou hast taken thyself off, thou strange fellow; I shall certainly not follow thee." But of the magical power which had been bestowed on his knapsack, he thought no more.

Brother Lustig traveled about with his money, and squandered and wasted what he had as before. When at last he had no more than four kreuzers, he passed by an inn and thought, "The money must go," and ordered three kreuzers' worth of wine and one kreuzer's worth of bread for himself. As he was sitting there drinking, the smell of roast goose made its way to his nose. Brother Lustig looked about and peeped, and saw that the host had two geese standing in the oven. Then he remembered that his comrade had said that whatsoever he wished to have in his knapsack should be there, so he said, "Oh, ho! I must try that with the geese."

So, he went out, and when he was outside the door, he said, "I wish those two roasted geese out of the oven and in my knapsack," and when he had said that, he unbuckled it and looked in, and there they were inside it. "Ah, that's right!" said he, "now I am a made man!" and went away to a meadow and took out the roast meat.

When he was in the midst of his meal, two journeymen came up and looked at the second goose, which was not yet touched, with hungry eyes. Brother Lustig thought to himself, "One is enough for me," and called the two men up and said, "Take the goose, and eat it to my health." They thanked him, and went with it to the inn, ordered themselves a half bottle of wine and a loaf, took out the goose which had been given them, and began to eat. The hostess saw them and said to her husband, "Those two are eating a goose; just look and see if it is not one of ours, out of the oven."

The landlord ran thither, and behold the oven was empty! "What!" cried he, "you thievish crew, you want to eat goose as cheap as that? Pay for it this moment, or I will wash you well with

148

green hazel-sap." The two said, "We are no thieves, a discharged soldier gave us the goose, outside there in the meadow."

"You shall not throw dust in my eyes that way! The soldier was here -- but he went out by the door, like an honest fellow. I looked after him myself; you are the thieves and shall pay!" But as they could not pay, he took a stick and cudgelled them out of the house.

Brother Lustig went his way and came to a place where there was a magnificent castle, and not far from it a wretched inn. He went to the inn and asked for a night's lodging, but the landlord turned him away, and said, "There is no more room here, the house is full of noble guests."

"It surprises me that they should come to you and not go to that splendid castle," said Brother Lustig.

"Ah, indeed," replied the host, "but it is no slight matter to sleep there for a night; no one who has tried it so far has ever come out of it alive."

"If others have tried it," said Brother Lustig, "I will try it too."

"Leave it alone," said the host, "it will cost you your neck."

"It won't kill me at once," said Brother Lustig, "just give me the key, and some good food and wine." So, the host gave him the key, and food and wine, and with this Brother Lustig went into the castle, enjoyed his supper, and at length, as he was sleepy, he lay down on the ground, for there was no bed.

He soon fell asleep, but during the night was disturbed by a great noise, and when he awoke, he saw nine ugly devils in the room, who had made a circle, and were dancing around him. Brother Lustig said, "Well, dance as long as you like, but none of you must come too close." But the devils pressed continually nearer

149

to him, and almost stepped on his face with their hideous feet. "Stop, you devil's ghosts," said he, but they behaved still worse.

Then Brother Lustig grew angry, and cried, "Hola! But I will soon make it quiet," and got the leg of a chair and struck out into the midst of them with it. But nine devils against one soldier were still too many, and when he struck those in front of him, the others seized him behind by the hair and tore it unmercifully. "Devil's crew," cried he, "it is getting too bad, but wait. Into my knapsack, all nine of you!" In an instant, they were in it, and then he buckled it up and threw it into a corner.

After this, all was suddenly quiet, and Brother Lustig lay down again and slept till it was bright day. Then came the innkeeper and the nobleman to whom the castle belonged, to see how he had fared; but when they perceived that he was merry and well they were astonished, and asked, "Have the spirits done you no harm, then?"

"The reason why they have not," answered Brother Lustig, "is because I have got the whole nine of them in my knapsack! You may once more inhabit your castle quite tranquilly, none of them will ever haunt it again." The nobleman thanked him, made him rich presents, and begged him to remain in his service, and he would provide for him as long as he lived. "No," replied Brother Lustig, "I am used to wandering about, I will travel farther."

Then he went away, and entered into a smithy, laid the knapsack, which contained the nine devils on the anvil, and asked the smith and his apprentices to strike it. So, they smote with their great hammers with all their strength, and the devils uttered howls which were quite pitiable. When he opened the knapsack after this, eight of them were dead, but one which had been lying in a fold of it was still alive, slipped out, and went back again to hell.

150

Thereupon Brother Lustig traveled a long time about the world, and those who know can tell many a story about him, but at last, he grew old and thought of his end, so he went to a hermit who was known to be a pious man, and said to him, "I am tired of wandering about, and want now to behave in such a manner that I shall enter into the kingdom of Heaven."

The hermit replied, "There are two roads, one is broad and pleasant, and leads to hell, the other is narrow and rough, and leads to heaven."

"I should be a fool," thought Brother Lustig, "if I were to take the narrow, rough road."

So, he set out and took the broad and pleasant road, and at length came to a great black door, which was the door of Hell. Brother Lustig knocked, and the doorkeeper peeped out to see who was there. But when he saw Brother Lustig, he was terrified, for he was the very same ninth devil who had been shut up in the knapsack and had escaped from it with a black eye.

So, he pushed the bolt in again as quickly as he could, ran to the devil's lieutenant, and said, "There is a fellow outside with a knapsack, who wants to come in, but as you value your lives don't allow him to enter, or he will wish the whole of hell into his knapsack. He once gave me a frightful hammering when I was inside it."

So, they called out to Brother Lustig that he was to go away again, for he should not get in there! "If they won't have me here," thought he, "I will see if I can find a place for myself in Heaven, for I must be somewhere."

So, he turned about and went onwards until he came to the door of Heaven, where he knocked. St. Peter was sitting hard by as doorkeeper. Brother Lustig recognized him at once, and thought,

"Here I find an old friend, I shall get on better." But St. Peter said, "I really believe that thou wantest to come into Heaven."

"Let me in, brother; I must get in somewhere; if they would have taken me into Hell, I should not have come here."

"No," said St. Peter, "thou shalt not enter."

"Then if thou wilt not let me in, take thy knapsack back, for I will have nothing at all from thee."

"Give it here, then," said St. Peter. Then Brother Lustig gave him the knapsack into Heaven through the bars, and St. Peter took it and hung it up beside his seat.

Then said Brother Lustig, "And now I wish myself inside my knapsack," and in a second he was in it, and in Heaven, and St. Peter was forced to let him stay there.

The Barn Owl's Talon

Once upon a time, there was a woman whom people said could read the future by "throwing the bones." It was said that she learned to do that from her mother, who learned it from her mother, who learned it from her mother, who learned it from her mother, who learned it from her mother, who unfortunately was hanged for being a witch. Thankfully, this great, great, great-granddaughter, now lived in a time of enlightenment where any religious or psychic inclination was tolerated as long as it didn't include someone dying as part of the ritual. That was still frowned upon by all of society, especially by those who identified themselves as part of the metaphysical world. They were very aware of the intolerance of the past and did not want it resurrected in any way, and thus, those who practiced mysticism followed those guidelines.

The woman was known throughout the community as Minerva, and whenever someone came to see her for the first time, she would explain to them everything that would take place during the reading. She told them that throwing the bones was an ancient tradition where those with psychic abilities would be able to use bones, along with other important items they had amassed over time, to provide answers to their questions. She always warned them that "the bones don't lie" and advised that they should not ask her questions unless they were ready to hear the answers. Though all of the first-time visitors said they understood, most of them failed to heed her warning.

She started each session by showing them the divination box, which was a square metal canister with rusted hinges that suggested the lid would not open, but it always did. Within the box was a throwing cloth, which was a black cloth with two yellow rings in the center of it, and numerous other items, that included a human finger bone, a squirrel bone, two small shells, a ring, a pearl earring, an old penny, three different colored crystals, the tiny hands and feet of a doll, a small fragment of petrified wood, several different sizes and colors of buttons, and a bottle cap. She then showed them the dark ivory talon, which she said came from a barn owl and was her token, and a small anvil-shaped bone that would be their token.

When she was asked about the anvil bone, she knew that a good reading would take place that day. She liked explaining to them why the anvil bone represented them and then watching the expressions on their faces. That reaction told her something about the person who was sitting across from her. If their eyes dilated as if all the light had been taken out of the room when they learned that the anvil bone came from the ear of a small blind child who had died over a hundred years ago, it meant they were intrigued by the spirit world. For those who sat there unblinking and whose eyes didn't change, she knew that they didn't understand the significance of the bone and would gain little insight from the reading.

After explaining everything to her visitors, she closed the lid on the divination box and would ask the individual to place their hands on it along with her, and together they would pray. They could pray about anything and to anyone but they had to do so in silence as she would be praying silently too. Minerva always asked the spirits of the natural world to assist her in the reading at that moment in time and she promised them she would always honor and respect the world in which she lived.

After completing the prayers, Minerva would open the box and dump the contents, without the barn owl talon, onto the cloth. Then she would sit and stare at the items until she had an understanding of what they were revealing. At that time, she would let her visitor know that they could ask her eleven questions and thus the reading would begin.

Those who had failed to understand the significance of the anvil bone always asked the same general questions about the same general subjects: money, work, marriage, and health. And the questions were almost always in that order. She never could understand why health was not among the first of their concerns, but she wasn't even sure she was helping them anyway. They heard what they wanted to hear and heard no more.

Those who had understood the significance of the anvil, seldom asked the same questions, though similar subject matter was usually addressed in some indirect manner. She took time to tell those individuals that all the items in the inner circle next to the anvil bone had a strong influence on the way they asked questions and on how she answered them. Those items that were in the outer circle still influenced their questions and her response, but because of their location to her spirit token, there was less certainty with her answer. If there was anything outside the two circles, she told them, the spirits had decided that those items would be of no value to either of them that day.

There were a few times that she just had to tell people that she could not answer the question they asked, but most of those times, it was with people who had no connection to the anvil bone. Seldom did that occur with those who had a spiritual affinity of some kind. She was always happy to tell someone that the crystals suggested a long and healthy life or that the illness that they or a loved one currently encountered would be overcome. She loved telling them that the buttons suggested they would not have money issues or the problem that gave them anxious moments now, would soon go away.

It was very hard for her to restrain the way she felt when she saw the tiny doll's hand and the ring or pearl earring next to the anvil bone. The words flowed out of her mouth and seemed to linger for a moment around the person's ears as they heard about how important family was in their life and that it would be filled with love and, at times, magic. It was just as magical for her to say those words for when she did, she truly felt connected to the women of her past.

There were also other times that there was indeed magic in the air, but it was a dark magic that caused a coldness inside her body that took days for her to dispel, and sometimes she suffered so much that she had to remain next to the fire to receive any comfort. Those were the times that she sensed evil sat across from her. She was never wrong. The tiny doll's feet were in the inner circle and the penny was tail side up. Though the questions they asked never betrayed their evil intent, she had to work hard not to display fear or in any way encourage them down the path that they had chosen.

Not that she could have changed things. The bones told the truth. And even though she believed they were fated to listen to the words of the old one and would not be able to ignore their wanton desires, it was only when she saw the fragment of the petrified wood within the small circle that she took action. The petrified wood next to the feet and penny could not be ignored. The old one was present in them now and if she didn't act, someone would die.

To those individuals, she always gave them a silver five-pronged star, and never once did they ask why. They liked the item because for them, it looked like a pentagram and they were drawn to it. It was not a pentagram but she knew how their minds worked and what they would think. She actually made them from finding old ball and jack games in antique stores and then filing off one of the prongs of the metal jacks and re-plating it with silver.

Once the silver five-pronged stars had been made, Minerva placed them in a barn owl's nest and waited. If the owl allowed it to stay there during nesting season, she knew it had spiritual powers which she enhanced through days of meditation and prayer. If it was tossed out, she threw them away as they would have no spiritual connection to her or nature. If they remained in the nest after nesting season and the owl returned to the nest to roost, she knew it had even greater power. She saved those particular stars for the most depraved of her clients.

She would give them the item and wait. And always, within two days, the person receiving it would die in a terrible accident. She didn't have to read the name of the person in the articles that she saw online. It wasn't necessary. Once she read how the person died, she knew.

Sometimes they had hung the silver star from the rearview mirror and the sun reflected off it into their eyes and would blind them for a moment as they drove their car into a tree or rock, or swerved into the other lane and in front of a sixteen-wheeler. Sometimes they hung it around their neck and got distracted as they rubbed and admired it, not noticing where they were going; falling off the side of a hill and crushing their head on a rock, or being impaled by the iron post of a fence. Sometimes they were killed in a terrible construction site accident. It didn't matter. They died a horrible death because they were focused on the silver star instead of the world around them.

It was after a reading with a person who required one of the most powerful stars she had, that she felt ill for several days. Her body was drained of energy and for a day and a half, all she did was lay in bed. But she couldn't sleep, so she read. She meditated. She prayed. On the second evening, she forced herself outside and sat there, hoping nature would help her heal. It did. She heard the barn owl calling to her and knew she would be able to sleep that night.

Minerva drank her cup of tea with honey and absinthe and then lay down in bed. If someone came into her bedroom fifteen minutes later, they would have assumed she was dead because she didn't move and

156

was barely breathing. But she was not dead. She was in a seizure-like dream state and could see and hear everything, but could not move.

She found herself in a forest looking down at her hands and saw that they had become talons and that her arms were feathered. She was a barn owl, sitting atop a tree limb staring into the night. It wasn't dark for her though. Peering through the darkness she saw the smokey figures sitting in front of an old tree. She wasn't sure how far away they were or why their bodies were not more defined. Suddenly one of the greenish-black figures reached out with what appeared to be some kind of arm. At the end was a black hand with long spikey fingers and it grabbed a human leg and tossed it onto the fire.

She then noticed the piles of human arms and legs next to them, stacked up like logs. She screamed and then heard the screech of an owl. The darker figure turned toward her and she saw a black form within a black silhouette. *How is that possible*, she thought, but when she saw its eyes that glowed like lava and spit out bits of fire that sizzled as they fell onto the ground, she wondered no more.

"The old barn owl is not happy with our presence here, Abaddon. I am sure it does not like the smell of burned flesh or perhaps it is you. You do have a putrid odor that permeates the air."

"I wear a cologne that honors you, old one," the greenish-black figure said. The orange eyes disappeared as if the black figure had turned back around.

"They refer to you in the book as the King of Locusts or Abaddon the Destroyer. Which do you prefer, my loyal and debauched servant?"

"It matters not to me. I take many forms, as you know, so what matters a name?"

"You have grown wise over the past several thousand years. Throw some more legs and arms on the fire and see if that owl screeches again!"

Minerva watched the greenish-black smoke take more form and saw that it had many arm-like appendages now, which were all covered in blood and a yellow mucous that dripped to the ground. At the end of each arm, the hand was now more defined. Where fingers should be were white bones with long black nails resembling scythes at the ends. They scooped up the arms and legs and dropped them onto the fire that burst into red flames and consumed the darkness. Minerva flapped her feathered arms and screeched again.

"It seems to know that you have come for it, Abaddon."

157

"It is time. This delicious peach needs to grow in the garden within our home, most malevolent one. She has become a delightful serial killer. She kills without remorse but she is tiring. I think it is time we reveal to her the wonders of the new world in which she has gained passage."

"I am not sure, Abaddon. She is indeed a wonderful serial killer as you say and I can sense that she does tire, but she is not dead yet. She may kill a hundred more in the years she has left just because she believes that they will commit a heinous act of violence. She fails to remember, as I am afraid you do, about the little caveat that He allows to rule this carnival. This experiment of His called 'free will' has created quite the irony and I do love irony. Killing those that you think could become evil is after all, quite evil and it pleases me greatly.

"I don't know what the future will hold my dear, twisted Abaddon. I have studied the prophets and the final story and I do know what is coming but I cannot see every day-to-day future event. I think we let her live a little longer. She may one day wake up and realize that no one she killed would have done anything evil and I think that will drive her mad. I know you can see how much fun that would be. Why collect our little peach now, when she bears such wonderful fruit in this garden? You could say she may stop. After all, she does have free will. I say yes, she does, so then why would she stop? Neither He nor I have intervened. She has no desire to stop, so she won't stop. Therefore, we let her continue her work here until she can go no more. That's what I wish, Abaddon."

"But what if she repents? They slip from our fingers when they repent, most wicked one. We would be risking that."

"True, but He is not the only one with the ability to resurrect life, provided we get here in time before He starts the firework show of white lights. We can show her the way then too, for am I not the great deceiver?"

"Yes. There are no equals."

"Thus, I say we leave her here. It is worth the risk. And if she escapes, well we have to admit, she was good to us. She sent us many because even though they may not have killed anyone, they wanted to and they forgot that little requirement of His before they died. Consequently, we did grow our garden because of our little peach owl regardless of His damn free will."

158

She heard the greenish-black thing moan and immediately felt the hot wind on her face as it tried to knock her off the limb, but she turned her head backward and dug her talons into the tree.

"Work with her some more, Abaddon. Entice her with some spell-books or some visions of those that she kills. Let her feel the power we can give her. Power is an aphrodisiac that few can ignore. Then we will have her and she cannot get away. Who knows? By then it may be the time that is written in the Book of Fables those followers of His cling to:

"'And the beast was given a mouth uttering haughty and blasphemous words, and it was allowed to exercise authority for forty-two months.....'"

"Really? I have never heard in all my days, someone in Hell call me haughty. And forty-two months? Where does He get off designating forty-two months? Still pisses me off sometimes but you know what they say: 'Better to reign in Hell than to serve in Heaven,' eh, Abaddon?"

"'Paradise Lost' by John Milton. Beautiful words that reflect the truth."

"Yes, indeed, my thoughtful servant. Let's leave this place, Abaddon, and head farther south into the Bible Belt. I would like to be entertained by another snake handler and poison show."

"Yes, my grand tormentor. I love that part of the country. The deception that poses as religion is most intoxicating within that domain."

The black being, like smoke, began to rise into the air. It turned back toward Minerva and she saw the fiery eyes again, staring at her as it laughed. The laughter roared into the darkness and everything within the forest was being swallowed up into that sound. Just as she was about to disappear, she awoke.

She felt feverish and was drenched in sweat when she opened her eyes. She got up and made some white willow bark and Echinacea tea. She only recalled parts of the dream but the elements she remembered caused her to shiver. She knew these thoughts and her body fatigue must have stemmed from the reading of the last person and it would take some time to get over it. She would rest another day, cleanse her body with essential oils, and fast, hydrating with only willow bark and Echinacea tea and an occasional spoonful of honey before she let the public know she was once again open for business.

159

Minerva felt much better the next day and her first two readings were very positive ones, but she was still tentative and uneasy. She thought it was because she had started back too soon and then he walked into the room. As soon as she saw him, she knew what the bones would say when she threw them and she wasn't wrong. She was glad she had gone into the kitchen before she started the reading. They both smelled the gas filling up the room as she scratched her barn owl talon across the table creating a spark. She thought she heard an enraged howl just before the white lights blinded her, as the gas and the dynamite that he had strapped to his body blew the house into splinters of exquisite inimitability.

Simeli Mountain

O nce upon a time, there were two brothers; one was rich, the other poor. However, the rich one gave nothing to the poor one, who barely made a living as a grain dealer. Things often went so badly for him that he had no bread for his wife and children.

One day he was pushing his cart through the forest when off to the side he saw a large bare mountain. He had never seen it before, so he stopped and looked at it with amazement. While he was standing there he saw twelve tall wild men approaching. Thinking that they were robbers, he pushed his cart into the thicket, climbed up a tree, and waited to see what would happen.

The twelve men went to the mountain and cried out, "Mount Semsi, Mount Semsi, open up." The barren mountain immediately separated down the middle. The twelve men walked into it, and as soon as they were inside, it shut.

A little while later it opened again, and the men came out carrying heavy sacks on their backs. As soon as they were all back in the daylight they said, "Mount Semsi, Mount Semsi, close." Then the mountain went back together, and the entrance could no longer be seen. Then the twelve men went away.

When they were completely out of sight, the poor man climbed down from the tree. He was curious to know what secret was hidden in the mountain, so he went up to it and said, "Mount Semsi, Mount Semsi, open up," and the mountain opened up for him as well.

161

He went inside, and the entire mountain was a cavern full of silver and gold, and in the back of the cavern there lay great piles of pearls and sparkling jewels, piled up like grain. The poor man did not know what he should do, whether or not he could take any of these treasures for himself. At last, he filled his pockets with gold, but he left the pearls and precious stones lying where they were.

Upon leaving he too said, "Mount Semsi, Mount Semsi, close," and the mountain closed. Then he went home with his cart.

He no longer had any cares, for with his gold he could buy bread for his wife and children, and wine as well. He lived happily and honestly, gave to the poor, and did good for everyone. When he ran out of money he went to his brother, borrowed a bushel, and got some more money, but did not touch any of the very valuable things. When he wanted to get some more money for the third time he again borrowed the bushel from his brother. However, the rich man had long been envious of his brother's wealth and of the fine household that he had furnished for himself. He could not understand where the riches came from, and what his brother wanted with the bushel. Then he thought of a trap. He covered the bottom of the bushel with pitch, and when he got the bushel back a gold coin was sticking to it.

He at once went to his brother and asked him, "What have you been measuring in the bushel?"

"Wheat and barley," said the poor brother.

Then he showed him the gold coin and threatened that if he did not tell the truth he would bring charges against him before the court. The poor man then told him everything that had happened to him. The rich man immediately had his wagon hitched up and drove away, intending to do better than his brother had done and to bring back with him quite different treasures.

162

When he came to the mountain he cried out, "Mount Semsi, Mount Semsi, open up."

The mountain opened, and he went inside. There lay the riches all before him, and for a long time, he did not know what he should take hold of first. Finally, he took as many precious stones as he could carry. He wanted to carry his load outside, but as his heart and soul were entirely occupied with the treasures, he had forgotten the name of the mountain, and cried out, "Mount Simeli, Mount Simeli, open up."

But that was not the right name, and the mountain did not move, remaining closed instead. He became frightened, and the longer he thought about it the more he became confused, and all of the treasures were of no use to him.

In the evening the mountain opened up, and the twelve robbers came inside. When they saw him, they laughed and cried out, "Bird, we have you at last. Did you think we did not notice that you came here twice? We could not catch you then, this third time you shall not get out again."

He cried out, "I wasn't the one. It was my brother!"

But however much he begged for his life, and in spite of everything that he said, they cut off his head.

A Similar Mountain

Once upon a time, two men were experiencing one of the best trips they had ever encountered. Unconventional as it may be, it provided the men more pleasure and more color and unique landscapes than many people would ever experience. It was a beautiful spring day and they were lying on lounge chairs on top of a ten-story building in downtown Atlanta, after having ingested acid in the form of eight-way hits of windowpane. This was referred to in the medical community as a very strong version of Lysergic acid diethylamide or more commonly abbreviated as LSD.

"Dude, I can't feel my ears. Or anything on my face. Or my legs and arms or hands. But I don't care. The sky is purple and dark blue with yellow spirals and about six or seven suns. Dude, it looks like a painting."

"Yeah, it does look like a painting. Maybe you can't feel your ears because you cut them off to make that painting."

"What the hell?"

"You know, like the van dough boy."

When he heard his friend say that, he burst out laughing and his friend joined in. They laughed for five full minutes as they looked at the sky and then over at each other. Each time they looked at each other they laughed even harder. They laughed so hard their sides hurt and one of them said they needed a beer.

"We got beer up here, where?"

"Shit, Nolan, now you're a poet too. This acid is bringing out all your artistic talents."

Nolan and John laughed again and John got up and walked three feet toward the cooler, carefully maneuvering as if he was traversing a tightrope. It took him fifteen minutes to get to the cooler, open it, walk back along the tightrope and sit back down. He handed Nolan the beer and they popped the tops in unison and toasted each other.

"What were you doing over there?" Nolan asked.

"What do you mean?"

"Getting the beer. You looked like you were walking on a tightrope."

"Damn, I was but I thought I was the only one who could see it. You saw it too?"

"No, I didn't see any rope, just a black strip of tar on the roof. I think it's tar, but it's beginning to move now. Damn, that isn't a snake is it?"

"It's ok. Black snakes are good snakes. Protect us from the poisonous ones."

"You don't think it's pissed because you walked along its back?"

"No man. I was using my tippy toes," John said as he burst out laughing. Nolan laughed too and this continued again for another five minutes before they finished their beer.

"I hope you got enough beer in that cooler. We're going to be flying high today and we may need some liquid parachutes to help us get back on the ground."

"Liquid parachutes. Wow, man! Where do you come up with this stuff? You need to start writing it down."

"Fuck writing it. I'll just record it in my phone," Nolan said as he pressed voice memo on his phone. "Memo 1. Liquid Parachutes."

"We may solve the world's problems today."

"Hell, give everyone an eight-way hit of this shit and there wouldn't be any problems."

"Well, I don't know about that." John got up to walk back over to the cooler. This time he bent down and felt the black image on the rooftop and realized it was only tar and laughed. He picked up the cooler and brought it over next to his chair and got him and his friend another one. "Some folks couldn't take this shit. They couldn't handle it like we can. Their minds are too messed up. You know, like Manson."

"Which one - Marilyn or Charles?"

"Dude, does it matter?"

"Ha! Good point. Hey, do you remember how we got on top of this mountain?"

John looked around at the rocky surface on which they were sitting and he couldn't remember how they did get up there. "Shit, no. But I know it's your mountain. In Hotlantis."

"Oh, yeah. It's my parent's old hotel, the Smoky Mountain Lodge Hotel. Cool place. Like our own little mountain top downtown."

165

"Yeah, I know, but how did we get up here and how do we get down?"

"I remember now. We came up through that door over there; the one that gets big and small and big and then small again."

John sat up and looked where Nolan was pointing and saw the door grow in size and then get so small that it looked like it belonged on a dollhouse.

"Well, we're going to have to get through it when it's big soon, 'cause we're going to run out of beer in about an hour or so."

"Damn, I don't want to be caught in that door when it changes size. Let's check out the side of this building and see if there are some ladders leading down to the bottom."

"Good idea," John said and they walked over to the edge of the rooftop. Down below they saw an alley, devoid of life except for a few people walking around looking into the trash cans.

"Those people down there look like ants. We must be pretty high."

"Truer words could not have been spoken," John said and they began laughing again. Nolan stumbled forward but John caught him and pulled him back and they stepped away from the edge of the rooftop and finished off their beer.

Nolan pulled out his phone and pushed voice memo again. "Memo 2. Canned foam pillows for your backpack when hiking."

"That is a fucking great idea. Now, that right there, might save someone."

"Yeah. But in the meantime, what do we do about beer?"

"You stay here and let me look over the side of the building again and see what I can figure out."

John walked back to the rooftop edge and stared at the buildings that morphed and melted away into either piles of bricks or other kinds of mountains. That's when he saw someone go up to a large pile of red rocks and put his hand on the side of it. A door opened up and the man walked into it as the red wall reappeared behind him.

"Holy shit," John said as he staggered back toward Nolan. "I found a magic building across from your magic mountain top."

"What?"

"Yeah, I saw some little dude, like a hobbit of some kind, go up to a wall, put his hand on it and a door opened up and he went in and then the wall became a wall again. As if he wasn't ever there."

"You do realize you are tripping your brains off right now, don't you?"

166

"I am telling you, man, I saw it. I really saw it."

"Drink a beer and tell me again what you saw," Nolan said.

John explained everything he saw to Nolan and then convinced him they should go down there so he could take a look for himself. Nolan agreed, primarily because he had seen a red neon sign that blazed "Beer" like it was on fire in a store window adjacent to the magic door John had supposedly discovered. They waited for the rooftop door to get big and when it did, John opened it and they walked in and saw the steps.

"Man, I was hoping there were steps," John said and they laughed as they lurched down them, telling each other to be quiet and only laughing even more when one of them said it.

As they exited the building, they found themselves in the alley. John whispered to Nolan not to look in the faces of anyone that they saw, as they would change into something that would mess with their heads. Though Nolan tried not to, he couldn't help but look at a few and when he did, he saw their nose where their ear should be, and ear where their nose should be and only one eye as if their face was one dimensional. They both saw a cat jump off the top of the trashcan. As it jumped in turned into ten cats before reforming into one when it landed on the alley pavement.

"Damn," Nolan said and shook his head. "You're right. Don't look in the faces, don't look at cats, don't look at anything; just go toward that wall."

They crossed the alley and went to the area of the wall where John saw the hobbit man enter. He moved his hands all over the wall, pushing into it and within a few minutes, a door popped open. Nolan pushed John through it before it closed or anyone could see them. They fell into a dark hall and lay there on the floor for several minutes before they said anything.

"What the hell just happened?" Nolan asked.

"We walked into a magic mountain through a magic wall."

"How is that possible?"

"I think we have transformed our bodies into molecular beings that have no limits within this realm of solids."

"What?"

"I don't know, but we won't know anything just sitting here in the dark. It's kind of creepy in here," John said as he stood and then helped Nolan up. They walked down the dark halls until a light came on and they saw they were in a large room filled with shelves of metal boxes. John took one of the boxes and placed it on a table in the middle of the room. When they opened it, they both fell back into one of the shelves, knocking more metal boxes to the floor.

"Oh shit, man. We have entered into a magic mountain of dwarves. Look at all this money and the jewels and stuff."

Nolan picked up a stack of money and began counting it.

"10 K, man. These are stacks of ten thousand dollars. God only knows how much money is in here; in all of those unopened boxes and even on the floor. This is real, right?"

John picked up one of the white jewels and scratched it across the top of the metal tin. It made a deep ridge into the top. "Glass doesn't do that. This shit is for real. We need to get the fuck out of here. Before that dwarf man comes back and chops off our heads with one of his axes."

"You didn't tell me he was carrying an ax."

"I didn't see the ax but I've read enough stories to let me know that dwarves always have axes."

"Let's take some of this money and jewelry and get the hell out of here," Nolan said. "We need some beer money anyway."

"Well, unless time has changed while we've been in here, which is possible, beer stores prefer cash over jewelry. Man, let's just take about a hundred dollars and vamoose. They won't miss that and that amount of money won't cause the dragon to get angry."

"Dragon. You saw a dragon?"

"Not yet, but just like the ax, they go hand in hand with the dwarves and the magic mountain."

"This acid really brings out the inner Tolkien in you, doesn't it? Dwarf or no dwarf, you saw a thief of some size and a hundred dollars isn't enough for beer. Let's take a thousand. We are pretty damn high and we are going to drink a lot of beer."

"Agreed," John said and he counted out ten one-hundred-dollar bills and gave five to Nolan and put five in his pocket. As they walked out of the room, the light turned off, and once again they were in the dark hall.

"I don't remember it being this dark before. You think your dragon is waiting for us in the shadows?"

"I don't know. But the shadows are moving around a bit, don't you think? Maybe we came into a shadow convention?

"A shadow convention?"

"Yeah. Fans of 'Dark Shadows' this way. Oooooh. That's going to be a fairly empty room. Yes, ma'am. The Eye Shadow clinic is this way. Shadow Boxers this way. Oh, Overshadows over there. Foreshadow? Oh, I see there are just four of you. I should have guessed. You can go in with the 'Dark Shadows' fans; at least there will be five of you in attendance then."

Nolan burst out laughing at John's description and just as it had done all day, it triggered more laughter from John. And as they laughed, they stumbled forward until they came back to the door, which opened and led them into the alley. Nolan said they needed to gain their composure before going into the beer store and getting a couple of cases and John agreed. They both wiped their hands down across their face to eradicate their laughing but when they saw each other do that, they started laughing again. It took them five times before the moving hand gesture worked and they had control of their laughter, at least for the moment.

They did not see the man who was watching them from the shadows. He wasn't sure what drugs they were doing but he could tell they were really messed up. *Easy targets*, he thought and he followed them into the store. He saw John pull out the five one-hundred-dollar bills and pay for the cases with a hundred, telling the cashier to keep the change. The cashier told John thanks and then said for the two of them to be careful. They said they would be fine as soon as they got back on top of their mountain. The cashier just smiled as they left the store.

The other man in the store walked to the window by the lottery tickets and watched John and Nolan enter the back door of the old hotel carrying the cases of beer. He would be paying them a visit later that evening. *They will be so shit-faced, this will be easy money. Plus, they have something I need*, he thought as he walked over to the counter and bought a pack of cigarettes.

John and Nolan made it back up the steps without any problems, though they stopped to admire several colorful vortexes on the wall before they got back to their chairs. They loaded as much beer as they could in the cooler and sat back down. They watched the sunset, remarking how every crayon color was there in the sky as day turned into evening, and spent several hours naming them and trying to keep track of who named the most. When John got up to get another beer, he walked over to the edge of the rooftop to glance at the red magic mountain again and saw seven gnomes with their orange hats enter an even larger door. He tripped backward and fell.

Nolan rushed to see if he was okay and John reported that he had seen seven gnomes entering the magic mountain.

"Don't you mean dwarves?" Nolan asked as he laughed.

"No, these dudes were gnomes, because they had orange hats and they didn't look friendly at all."

"You saw the hats and their faces from up here in the dark?"

"I saw the fucking hats for sure, man. And I swear several of them looked up at me and they didn't look friendly."

"Maybe they were just constipated?" Nolan asked and then they both laughed uncontrollably at that thought until they saw the man standing there with a gun pointed at them.

"Oh, shit. Nolan. I'm not sure if I want you to tell me you see that or not, but tell me what you see."

"Don't need to answer him, Nolan. I am for real. I've been watching and waiting for you two acid heads to drink all that beer you bought. I see you've made a pretty good dent in it, but you are still too fucked up to understand, so let me make this perfectly clear. I want all your money and then I'll be gone and you two can continue to allow the universe and the stars to mystify you."

"No problem, dude," Nolan said as he handed him the five one-hundred-dollar bills.

"Good job, Nolan. Now you, I believe it is John, right? Give me your money."

"Sure man, sure, but I'm not going back into that mountain to get anymore. I just saw the gnomes go in there."

"The red mountain?"

John gave the man the money and nodded his head.

"You know. I've been watching that place for a week and haven't been able to get in there yet. But you somehow got in."

"Yeah, I just put my hand on the wall and a door opened up. But you don't want to go in there now. The gnomes are in there. You don't want to fuck with gnomes. "

"Yeah, I'm sure they're in there as you say, but I'm not afraid of gnomes. Werewolves are what frighten me. Seeing how you didn't run into any of those, why don't you go down there with me and let me in, and then you can leave. And I'll take care of the gnomes."

"No, man. I gave you the money. I'm not fucking with the gnomes. There are way too many. They'll swarm both of us and then we'll both be dead."

"You know, it was one of your fingers that got you in the magic mountain. Which finger do you think it was?" the man asked.

John raised his middle finger and smiled but the man grabbed his hand and cut off his thumb with some very sharp garden shears before John or Nolan could even move.

"I feel a lightning bolt in my hand and I can see the blood cells, Nolan. I can see the red blood cells, the white blood cells, and the platelets. It's fucking cool," John said as he and Nolan watched the blood dripping onto the ground. Though his neural pathways were still greatly altered, Nolan's first aid response was an instinctive one, as he retrieved some ice and then wrapped his shirt around the ice and John's hand. The man disappeared out the door and neither John nor Nolan ever saw him leave.

It's always the thumb with these biometric devices. I knew that fucker would say no, the man thought as he walked down the steps. He would still be surprised if John's thumb worked because he also knew the biometric systems needed about an eighty percent match to activate them. When he stood next to the wall, he placed John's thumb into the bricks in a systematic manner. Within about ten minutes, he felt the thumb move slightly into the brick and watched as the door opened.

Ha! I knew it was my lucky day when I won fifty dollars on that two-dollar scratcher at the beer store. One more black eight or Jack, and I would have won fifty thousand dollars. But I guess all I needed was a thumb, the man chuckled to himself. Walking down the dark corridor, he pulled out his gun and then moved into the great room when the overhead light was activated.

He saw the truck and the traffic cones behind it and thought about what John had said about the gnomes. "Shit. He was all fucked up," he muttered as he laughed out loud and looked at the money and the jewelry lying on the floor. He then noticed all the red dots on his body and heard someone tell him not to move.

Out of the shadows, came seven men, all carrying automated weapons and looking angrily at him. A man wearing sunglasses came over to him and placed the barrel tip of a .45 automatic to his head.

"Okay, so you're the fuck that got in here and started going through all our stuff. Not cool, man. How the hell did you do it?"

The intruder showed him the thumb and the man with the sunglasses looked at it and then at the stranger's intact hands.

"Whose thumb is this?" the man with the sunglasses asked as he removed his glasses and took hold of the severed thumb.

"Some acid head. Over there on the rooftop drinking beer and becoming one with the universe." As soon as he said those words, the intruder's eyes widened with familiarity as he saw the smile.

"I'll be damned. That sounds like John. I didn't even know he was back in town. Last time I heard from him he was in Colorado howling at the moon with some Zuni shaman. We sort of grew apart over a woman, about two years ago. Stupid of us to do that. I said some things I regret and he said some things he regrets but we just parted ways after that, and then I got that postcard from Colorado. He apologized and said he wanted to get together, but just like him, he didn't call. I bet he's up there on the rooftop with Nolan, isn't he? On top of Nolan's parents' old hotel. Empty hotel but still cool-looking and expensive real estate. Ah, don't answer that. I'll find out soon enough. Oh, and I don't suppose by chance, my twin brother just gave you his thumb, did he?"

The man didn't say a word or move a muscle.

"You are a fucking thief, which isn't a problem for me because I am a fucking thief. But you also harmed an innocent man who just likes to get high. Dude, this isn't going to be a good day for you. You are a rat and you know what we do with rats? We put them in a room with other rats. Frank, take this man, I don't even want to know his name, and put him in the rat room. If you survive forty-eight hours in there with them, you can leave. If you don't, well then, you don't. Either way, you have learned a good lesson. Don't fuck with a man's brother and another man's money, especially if that other man likes to steal things and play with guns and is very good at both of them. By the way, rats without a food source will just eat other rats."

The man was thrown into a dark room with a hundred hungry sewer rats, some of them as big as a dachshund. He was already screaming as they locked the metal door.

"Thank you, Frank. Why don't you and the other men, count up what we just took from that friendly credit union, and I'll go across the street and say hello to my brother and his friend. I told him he'd hurt himself

172

one day up on that roof doing acid. I guess this just proves my point."
He smiled, picked up the thumb, and put it into a cup of ice.

"Maybe this thumb can help mend our relationship. John would like
that analogy. Even as fucked up as I know he is, he'll get a kick out of
it," he said as he laughed and walked down the corridor.

Rumpelstiltskin

Once upon a time, there was a miller who was poor, but who had a beautiful daughter. Now it happened that he got into a conversation with the king, and to make an impression on him he said, "I have a daughter who can spin straw into gold."

The king said to the miller, "That is an art that I really like. If your daughter is as skillful as you say, then bring her to my castle tomorrow, and I will put her to the test."

When the girl was brought to him, he led her into a room that was entirely filled with straw. Giving her a spinning wheel and a reel, he said, "Get to work now. Spin all night, and if by morning you have not spun this straw into gold, then you will have to die." Then he himself locked the room, and she was there all alone.

The poor miller's daughter sat there, and for her life, she did not know what to do. She had no idea how to spin straw into gold. She became more and more afraid and finally began to cry.

Then suddenly the door opened. A little man stepped inside and said, "Good evening, Mistress Miller, why are you crying so?"

"Oh," answered the girl, "I am supposed to spin straw into gold, and I do not know how to do it."

The little man said, "What will you give me if I spin it for you?"

"My necklace," said the girl.

The little man took the necklace, sat down before the spinning wheel, and whir, whir, whir, three times pulled, and the spool was full. Then he put another one on, and whir, whir, whir, three times pulled, and the second one was full as well. So it went until morning, and then all the straw was spun, and all the spools were filled with gold.

At sunrise, the king came, and when he saw the gold he was surprised and happy, but his heart became even more greedy for gold. He had the miller's daughter taken to another room filled with straw. It was even larger, and he ordered her to spin it in one night if she valued her life.

The girl did not know what to do, and she cried. Once again, the door opened, and the little man appeared. He said, "What will you give me if I spin the straw into gold for you?"

"The ring from my finger," answered the girl.

The little man took the ring and began once again to whir with the spinning wheel. By morning he had spun all the straw into glistening gold. The king was happy beyond measure when he saw it, but he still did not have his fill of gold. He had the miller's daughter taken to a still larger room filled with straw, and said, "Tonight you must spin this too. If you succeed you shall become my wife." He thought, "Even if she is only a miller's daughter, I will not find a richer wife in all the world."

When the girl was alone the little man returned for a third time. He said, "What will you give me if I spin the straw this time?"

"I have nothing more that I could give you," answered the girl.

"Then promise me, after you are queen, your first child."

"Who knows what will happen," thought the miller's daughter, and not knowing what else to do, she promised the little man what he demanded. In return, the little man once again spun the straw into gold.

When in the morning the king came and found everything just as he desired, he married her, and the beautiful miller's daughter became queen.

A year later she brought a beautiful child into the world. She thought no more about the little man, but suddenly he appeared in her room and said, "Now give me that which you promised."

The queen took fright and offered the little man all the wealth of the kingdom if he would let her keep the child, but the little man said, "No. Something living is dearer to me than all the treasures of the world."

Then the queen began lamenting and crying so much that the little man took pity on her and said, "I will give you three days time. If by then you know my name, then you shall keep your child."

The queen spent the entire night thinking of all the names she had ever heard. Then she sent a messenger into the country to inquire far and wide what other names there were. When the little man returned the next day, she began with Kaspar, Melchior, Balzer, and said in order all the names she knew. After each one, the little man said, "That is not my name."

The second day she sent inquiries into the neighborhood as to what names people had. She recited the most unusual and most curious names to the little man: "Is your name perhaps Beastrib? Or Muttoncalf? Or Legstring?"

But he always answered, "That is not my name."

On the third day the messenger returned and said, "I have not been able to find a single new name, but when I was approaching a high mountain in the corner of the woods, there where the fox and the hare say good-night, I saw a little house. A fire was burning in front of the house, and an altogether comical little man was jumping around the fire, hopping on one leg and calling out:

> "Today I'll bake; tomorrow I'll brew,
> Then I'll fetch the queen's new child,
> It is good that no one knows,
> Rumpelstiltskin is my name."

You can imagine how happy the queen was when she heard that name. Soon afterward the little man came in and asked, "Now, Madame Queen, what is my name?"

She first asked, "Is your name Kunz?"

"No."

"Is your name Heinz?"

"No."

"Is your name perhaps Rumpelstiltskin?"

"The devil told you that! The devil told you that!" shouted the little man, and with anger, he stomped his right foot so hard into the ground that he fell in up to his waist. Then with both hands, he took hold of his left foot and ripped himself up the middle in two.

Stilts

Once upon a time, a wicked child was born. Some believed that he was just a product of his environment and his wickedness arose from the lack of love he received because he was ridiculed from the moment he was born. But many children are teased or mocked for one thing or another and they don't become evil, hence, some believed that theory was flawed. Some believed that the child was just born evil, and as time would tell, their beliefs would be proven true.

Even so, the derision and uncaring words did help frame the evil that was evident in the child. He was born with ears that were so big they had to be folded over to allow the child to emerge from the birth canal. Kind people who saw ears that size on a baby would say, "Don't worry, he'll grow into them." But in this particular case, the child's head would have had to grow to the size of a watermelon. So, no one said anything like that.

He was also born with a large crooked nose that only grew larger and more crooked as he got older. And without a doubt, he had the thinnest of lips that any of the medical staff had ever seen. They were more like slits of skin that merely outlined the upper row of little jagged yellow teeth from the bottom row of little jagged yellow teeth.

Yes, this child had teeth at birth. It is rare but it does happen and it only encouraged the word "goblin" when people described his appearance. The mother only saw the baby once before she snuck away from the hospital. She was so disturbed by the child's appearance that she had to leave before she heard them curse her for its birth, or before those of similar ilk came looking for her and the baby.

His arms were of normal length for a newborn baby but his hands were not. They were very big with long bony fingers. The nurses said his hands looked like "daddy long leg spiders" and recoiled each time he reached for them. His tiny stumps for legs only exacerbated the odd appearance of the child as nothing about him, besides his arms, appeared normal. People instinctively turned away when they saw him.

History will state that no child is born with black eyes, that the iris is only a very, very dark brown. But no one would dispute the medical personnel's belief that this child had eyes that were black. "Black as coal" or "black as tar" were phrases that were used frequently to reference the child's eyes and the nursing staff encouraged the hospital administration to find a place for this child as soon as possible.

Social workers tried to place the child, but once it was seen, it was rejected by all the agencies. All hope was lost that the child would ever leave the facility and soon everything bad that happened within its walls was blamed upon the child's presence. Infection and mortality rates increased, and staff morale plummeted. Smart men and women of science knew that their science could not overcome what surrounded that child. Just before one nurse took it upon herself to correct the problem, a woman came into the hospital and announced she would take the child.

The hospital administration did not know where the woman came from and did not question the fact that she was old and perhaps blind. They allowed her to sign the paperwork that granted her legal custody and happily escorted her and the child to the door. The hospital workers all said that the woman was an angel of mercy. That made them feel better about themselves, but in reality, they knew the woman was more likely an emissary from the Devil.

The woman was a distant relative of an employee of the hospital and had heard the therapist speak of the "goblin" child and was intrigued by its description. Because she had known other people with unique characteristics in her lifetime, she knew a place to take the child and, at the same time, make herself rich. She was not completely blind and when she saw the child, she knew her instincts would be proven right.

It had once been a famous circus and was one of the few that still traveled across the country to perform. The child was welcomed into their group and the woman was employed to oversee his development.

The circus people knew the child was special and were not afraid of his attributes that hinted at a relationship with a darker power. They knew how to promote that type of story to their advantage, once the child was old enough to perform and garner an interested audience.

The old woman, whose name was Cosmina, named the child Rupert and he grew strong with her care and guidance. The facial features of the baby did not change much as the boy aged. The main difference was that the teeth the baby was born with had been replaced with permanent teeth, if you could call them teeth at all. He never had a full set even when fully grown but that could be considered a blessing. The pieces of enameled daggers he did have, could pull leather apart. They provided him sufficient ability to eat, but also the capacity to be used as a weapon when required. His spiderish hands grew strong with a vise-like grip, and his stumps became sturdy legs that were extremely flexible.

Cosmina delighted in Rupert's growth and his acceptance of the surroundings in which he now lived. To him, she was his mother even though she told him when he was old enough to understand, that his birth mother had deserted him and she had come for him. When he asked her why she wanted him when no one else did, she told him that she could see what others didn't. She was made different from other human babies too and people like them made the world more special because of their presence. Rupert was enchanted by Cosmina's words and he savored them each time he heard her repeat them, which she did often.

All of the circus acts helped tutor Rupert, but one was more influential than the others; a man named Daka, who was known as the Delhi Demon. Daka felt no pain. He could lay on a bed of nails, drive nails into his hand or his nose, and could wrap his arms and legs completely around his neck. He taught Rupert many tricks about dislocating a limb without damaging it and how not to hurt oneself when placing sharp objects into your body. He also instructed him in the use of makeup to enhance his menacing look.

Daka had never seen a child learn so rapidly and he suggested to Cosmina that he could be the only person in the world to do a high wire act on large stilts. Rupert loved the idea and he worked tirelessly with Daka and the Hungarian high wire walker known as Gergo the Magnificent. At first, Rupert simply walked among the crowds on his stilts, frightening young children as he bent down to look into their eyes with his black ones, emphasized with red and yellow makeup. And when he smiled, the mother or father usually recoiled from seeing the horrific face move toward them as he made a menacing noise with his throat that sounded like a choked cat. Rupert relished the power his appearance yielded and the tingling feeling that came over his body when he scared people. He continued to work with Gerko many hours each day to learn how to perform on the high wire while on stilts, knowing that he would have more power over people's feelings when he was doing something that they could not imagine any human could accomplish.

When Rupert turned fifteen, he was promoted for the first time as one of the premier acts of the circus. He was called the "Flying Goblin" and when he went out onto the high wire in the spotlights, people were mesmerized. He moved from one end of the wire to the other and even jumped up and down on those stilts to the gasps of the crowd. Rupert could feel the emotions of every person watching him as if they were shots injected into his body, and like drugs, they triggered a feeling of euphoria and invincibility. And when he heard a gasp or scream, the sense of that primal fear produced a scent that wafted through his nostrils which was stimulating and addictive.

By the time he was eighteen, Rupert was the star of the high wire act and the "Flying Goblin" had added a new twist to his performance. Not only was it advertised as "death-defying" because he was doing a high wire act on stilts without a net, but he also now executed it over a cage containing several large alligators. The fact that there were alligators in a cage created an illusion of danger and fear among the spectators, but Rupert and Daka knew that alligators seldom attacked people on land. However, Rupert practiced jumping off the high wire in case that was ever needed and was soon capable of landing from a height of twenty feet without injuring himself. He had an amazing ability to withstand pain when his stilted legs hit the ground, and should the alligator decide it did want to attack him, Rupert always carried two weapons: a large knife that could cut through the alligator's tough hide, and his teeth, which were just as dangerous as those that the alligator possessed.

Rupert began the show by entering the tent in total darkness, carrying a large flashlight with him. The whispers of the crowd grew with each second as the crowd wondered where he was. A light would flash erratically, followed by erupting screams. The tension grew with each step he took and no one was aware of his presence until there would be another flash of light which outlined Rupert's nightmarish face looking down at a terrified spectator from a body that was over ten feet in the air.

People loved being scared and Rupert's shows became standing room only, but he wanted to experience even more fear from the crowds to satisfy the malignant craving that grew within him. When he asked Cosmina about other things he might try, she said something he didn't expect to hear. She reminded him of the day when she told him that she was also different and then explained to him that she was only half-human. The other half of her was produced by an incubus, a type of demon, and therefore, she had demon blood within her. Rupert smiled when he heard that and asked her if he too, was demon bred. Cosmina shook her head no and declared he was even more special and had been given a power that could truly bring even more fear to the humans.

Soon afterward, the circus advertised "The Flying Goblin" high wire act along with the chance to tempt fate by meeting with the Goblin after the act. For the mere cost of ten dollars, the Flying Goblin would allow them an opportunity to win a hundred dollars. If he failed to guess any part of their name, they would win the hundred dollars. And because Rupert, under Cosmina's tutelage, understood human nature, he would purposefully guess the wrong name of those people he knew would not take the next part of the challenge. They would walk away with the hundred dollars and in doing so, generate more excitement from others about responding to the dare.

He also guessed the wrong name of those he knew would take the next part of the challenge, which was a chance to win more money. All they had to do to double their money was guess something about him or his act that was not real. But if they failed in doing that, they would have to endure a curse that would harm them in some way. They never guessed correctly and Rupert was elated each time, knowing that person walked away cursed, and only he knew what form it would take and when it would happen. He treasured the ones who left saying they didn't "believe in curses." He always ensured what happened to them was most memorable and occurred when least expected.

The second part of the "Goblin Challenge" became very popular. Those who dared, asked all sorts of questions. When they guessed his nose wasn't real, he would allow them to touch it and watch as they

182

tried to restrain their displeasure at feeling something so odd and inhuman. If they speculated his teeth weren't real, he showed them how real they were by often asking to see their belt and then ripping it to shreds with his teeth. Many thought his ears weren't real, but when they touched them, he would wiggle his ears and laugh when they jumped back as if they had received an electric shock. If they guessed the stilts weren't real, he would let them examine them or his muscular stumps and feet which looked more like thick pads of flesh than feet.

People joked about "the curse" at first until strange things began to happen to those who had left the show cursed. Dairy farmers would suddenly find their cow's milk was more blood than milk. Bankers would have their banks robbed. Athletes would suffer broken bones. Housewives would burn themselves cooking or suffer a freak accident of some sort at home. But these incidents were usually only known by family members or friends, and so the awareness of the curse being real was not as widespread as that of winning money from the Flying Goblin. But Rupert always knew when bad things happened to those he had bedeviled.

While guessing names or answering questions, Rupert realized he had an opportunity to induce even more fear and awe among the spectators. He would claim he could drive a nail into his hand and not be injured and they would say he couldn't and watch when he did. He would tell them he could inhale blood into his nose and spit it out of his eyes and they would say he couldn't and then be disturbed when he shot the blood from his eyes onto their face or shirt. These were illusions that Daka had taught him and Rupert kept finding ways to do things people could not believe were possible.

He would catch an arrow in his giant spider-like hands while on the high wire. He would perform his high wire act over metal stakes sticking out of the ground or over poisonous snakes or fire and then people who would take the challenge would want to inspect the stakes or see if the snakes were real. And if they said the fire wasn't real, Rupert would light a torch and let them feel its heat before he stuck it down his throat and extinguished it only to relight it by regurgitating a volatile liquid he could keep in his stomach until he was ready to bring up out of his mouth.

The show became even more famous and Rupert and Cosmina became even richer. Rupert, however, grew to enjoy the curses he placed on people even more than the show itself and he wanted to make the curses harsher. Cosmina told him he would regret doing that but Rupert didn't care. He wanted to curse the people that had cursed him, and so people soon began to suffer more serious, and even at times, deadly accidents. With each death, the Flying Goblin's dare and curse became more notorious and people became more reluctant to take the challenge even when Rupert gave away more money or shoved more nails into his hand or nose.

Still, people came to the show because Rupert continued to make his aerial act even more dangerous. He would walk over large vats of acid that would burn, if not kill him if he fell into them. He would dodge more arrows shot at him while he was on the high wire and at times, he even let some of them go into his body, which he of course had prepared for, and was not injured. But the crowd didn't know that and they continued to come to the show and to gasp and scream. Though fewer took the challenge, there were still those who did, and they suffered greatly for their ignorance and greed. And Rupert reveled in the suffering he placed upon them.

As he was answering questions one night, he saw a man and his child watching and listening to everything he said from a distance. Finally, after everyone had left, they began to walk away but Rupert called them over and said he would give them a chance to win his money without even having to pay anything. The man just shook his head and said he didn't wish to participate. Rupert then looked at the little boy who wore braces on his legs and grinned devilishly. He had never cursed a child before. This one would bring him immense pleasure as he caused the boy even more agony. He told the little boy he could win one thousand dollars if he would only play, and the little boy just smiled and said, "I wish I had real legs like you." Hearing those words, Rupert screamed, "No!" and stood up.

The man and the boy watched as Rupert's legs unfolded from beneath his back until he towered over them. And then they watched the legs began to splinter and break apart, and with each break, Rupert screamed. For the fact was, Rupert's secret was that the stilts that he walked upon were not stilts at all; they were his real legs. As he had grown, so had his legs, until they were over seven feet in length and had several knee-like joints that held them together. Daka had taught him how to dislocate the joint and allow him to look as if he had only stumps for legs. The flesh that people mistook as his feet were just one of his padded knees that had developed over the years. While sitting and answering the people's questions, Rupert was able to fold his legs up behind him under the cape he wore during his act as the Flying Goblin. "It will be the greatest illusion of all time," Daka had told Cosmina. But for all things of this earth, time is not endless.

Cosmina had not told Rupert what would happen to him if someone guessed the secret because she was, after all, half-demon. Now that the secret was revealed, Rupert's joints burst open as if a pin had pierced a balloon filled with a vile liquid, and the segments of his bones broke apart one by one into millions of white and bloody splinters until all that remained was Rupert's torso. It was as if all the vessels in his body had exploded at the same time and all the blood drained out, and within a minute, there was nothing left but a wrinkled and putrid form of a malevolent being with a very ugly head, slumped over onto the ground.

The little boy and the man stood there for a moment until Cosmina walked up to them. She told the man that his child was special and asked if he would like for her to tutor him and expand his considerable mental abilities. She said his son could become very famous as his mind and intuitiveness were a rarity among men. The man just shook his head no. The son looked at Cosmina and said she should be worried because he knew what she was too. She said nothing else as she backed away and lowered her head until she was certain they were gone and never again returned to that part of the world.

Made in the USA
Monee, IL
31 July 2023

40230431R00108